英語 *Make Me High* 系列

# Vocabulary

## 4000
## Exercise Book

### 必考4000單字實戰題本

丁雍嫻 邢雯桂 盧思嘉 應惠蕙 編著
張淑娸 修訂

 三民書局

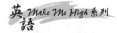

# Vocabulary 4000 Exercise Book
## ——必考 4000 單字實戰題本

| | |
|---|---|
| 編 著 者 | 丁雍嫻等 |
| 修 訂 者 | 張淑娸 |
| 創 辦 人 | 劉振強 |
| 發 行 人 | 劉仲傑 |
| 出 版 者 | 三民書局股份有限公司 (成立於 1953 年) |

三民網路書店
https://www.sanmin.com.tw

| | |
|---|---|
| 地　　址 | 臺北市復興北路 386 號　（復北門市）　(02)2500–6600 |
| | 臺北市重慶南路一段 61 號（重南門市）　(02)2361–7511 |
| 出版日期 | 初版一刷 2001 年 10 月 |
| | ⋮ |
| | 修訂二版一刷 2003 年 4 月 |
| | 修訂二版二十一刷 2024 年 9 月 |
| 書籍編號 | S804120 |
| I S B N | 978-957-14-3532-9 |

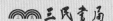

# 序

英語 Make Me High 系列的理想在於超越，在於創新。

這是時代的精神，也是我們出版的動力；

這是教育的目的，也是我們進步的執著。

針對英語的全球化與未來的升學趨勢，

我們設計了一系列適合普高、技高學生的英語學習書籍。

面對英語，不會徬徨不再迷惘，學習的心徹底沸騰，

心情好 High！

實戰模擬，掌握先機知己知彼，百戰不殆決勝未來，

分數更 High！

選擇優質的英語學習書籍，才能激發學習的強烈動機；

興趣盎然便不會畏懼艱難，自信心要自己大聲說出來。

本書如良師指引循循善誘，如益友相互鼓勵攜手成長。

展書輕閱，你將發現……

學習英語原來也可以這麼 High！

# 前　言

　　《Vocabulary 4000 Exercise Book——必考4000單字實戰題本》乃根據應考必備之4000個字彙範圍，由作者群模擬大考題型精心編寫而成。全書共分30回，每回皆含50個選擇題，題型包括以下三大類型：

一、**Vocabulary**（文意字彙選擇，20題）
　　測驗學生對英文單句的理解程度及各單字的熟悉度。

二、**Idioms and Phrases**（片語選擇，10題）
　　評量學生對詞組及慣用語的運用程度。

三、**Cloze Test**（克漏字選擇，20題）
　　了解學生掌握靈活運用單字之能力，進而將單字運用於完整之文章內。
透過這些題型，學生的字彙實力將可由點、線、面全方位地作評估。

　　本手冊的使用方式不拘。學生可先研讀本編輯部出版的《Vocabulary 4000——必考4000單字書》，於熟悉各單字之用法後再以本手冊驗收學習成果；亦可直接利用本手冊複習以前學過的單字，並檢視較不熟悉的單字及片語，利用其他工具書（如字典）的輔助，擴增自己的字彙。無論何種方式，相信皆能增強讀者們的字彙能力。

　　字彙乃語文之本，能通曉各單字的意義、掌握重要單字的用法，則各式題型的測驗皆不足為懼。期望本手冊能對正在準備考試的莘莘學子們有所助益。

三民英語編輯小組　謹誌

# Table of Contents

## I. Vocabulary

_____ 1. I need 3 _____ of paper for my assignment.

    (A) sheets     (B) loaves     (C) slices     (D) cartons

_____ 2. The illness is thought to be caused by a defective _____ rather than germs.

    (A) gene     (B) birth     (C) contact     (D) media

_____ 3. She slept only one hour last night; _____, she looks marvelously refreshed today.

    (A) therefore     (B) besides     (C) moreover     (D) nevertheless

_____ 4. The ship was sinking fast so the captain gave the order to _____ it.

    (A) dessert     (B) abandon     (C) drown     (D) absorb

_____ 5. Please don't _____ the thing to others. We have to keep it a secret.

    (A) adjust     (B) expect     (C) ignore     (D) reveal

_____ 6. It didn't take long before his wound _____ over.

    (A) cured     (B) consulted     (C) healed     (D) infected

_____ 7. After the _____ performance, all the audience stood up and applauded.

    (A) impressed     (B) marvelous     (C) humble     (D) ordinary

_____ 8. After Ben's house was broken into, the police asked him to make a list of the missing _____.

    (A) articles     (B) matters     (C) events     (D) circles

_____ 9. She decided to _____ herself on those who insulted her.

    (A) reveal     (B) revise     (C) review     (D) revenge

_____ 10. He _____ her silence as agreement.

    (A) transformed     (B) decided     (C) interpreted     (D) proved

_____ 11. A happy marriage must be based on _____ respect and understanding between husband and wife.

    (A) common     (B) double     (C) pair     (D) mutual

_____ 12. She paid her meal with a one-hundred-dollar _____.

    (A) paper     (B) bill     (C) bank     (D) deposit

_____ 13. The salt air _____ that the sea was not far away.

    (A) admitted     (B) remarked     (C) commanded     (D) suggested

_____ 14. Prof. Smith rarely got _____ involved with any female student.

    (A) generally     (B) emotionally     (C) logically     (D) frankly

_____ 15. Any language that has a hint on sexual or racial discrimination will be considered

_____ .

    (A) complimentary    (B) destructive    (C) respectful    (D) offensive

_____ 16. The newly-built stadium has a seating _____ of fifty thousand.

    (A) capacity    (B) reservation    (C) bench    (D) capability

_____ 17. She _____ the little girl 5 thousands for bringing back the lost kitty.

    (A) abandoned    (B) rewarded    (C) imitated    (D) affected

_____ 18. The medical _____ in this mountainous area are poor.

    (A) compositions    (B) charities    (C) facilities    (D) organizations

_____ 19. Young people tend to share their secrets with their _____ rather than with their parents.

    (A) pairs    (B) matches    (C) peers    (D) companies

_____ 20. I didn't have time to read the whole article so I just read the first _____ .

    (A) colony    (B) column    (C) code    (D) copy

## II. Idioms & Phrases

_____ 1. As the company is losing money, the management has decided to _____ some workers.

    (A) call off    (B) lay off    (C) put off    (D) pull off

_____ 2. I hope my teacher will _____ the fact that I was seriously ill when taking the test.

    (A) take into account    (B) gain access to    (C) take for granted    (D) make up her mind

_____ 3. We had _____ returned home _____ it rained.

    (A) no sooner...than    (B) better...than    (C) nothing...but    (D) would rather...than

_____ 4. Missing my plane was a blessing _____ because the plane crashed just after takeoff.

    (A) in disguise    (B) in disorder    (C) at will    (D) at ease

_____ 5. They managed to finish the difficult task _____ .

    (A) at width    (B) on width    (C) at length    (D) on length

_____ 6. After the war, they came back to find that their house had _____ .

    (A) burnt off    (B) burnt down    (C) burnt alive    (D) burnt to death

_____ 7. The knife _____ cut meat.

    (A) is used to    (B) get used to    (C) used to    (D) is used for

_____ 8. The thieves _____ before the police came.

    (A) got abroad    (B) got around    (C) got away    (D) got back

_____ 9. After the outdoor concert, the audience _____ great amounts of trash in the park.

    (A) left out     (B) left alone     (C) left for     (D) left behind

_____ 10. We decided to offer the job to Mr. Baker _____ other better applicants.

    (A) on account of     (B) in case of     (C) by way of     (D) in the absence of

## III. Cloze Test

### Part A

A friend of mine named Paul received an automobile from his brother as a Christmas present. On Christmas Eve when Paul came out of his office, a boy was walking around the shiny new car, admiring it. "Is this your car, Mister?" he asked.

Paul _____1_____. "My brother gave it to me for Christmas." The boy was astounded. "You _____2_____ your brother gave it to you for nothing? Boy, I wish...." He _____3_____.

Of course, Paul knew what he was going to wish for. He was going to wish he had a brother like that. But the boy went on, "I wish I could _____4_____ a brother like that."

Paul _____5_____ the boy in astonishment, then impulsively he added, "Would you like to take a ride in my car?"

"Oh, yes, I'd love that."

After a short ride, the boy turned and said, "Mister, would you _____6_____ driving in front of my house?" Paul thought he knew what the lad wanted. He wanted to show off to his _____7_____ that he could ride home in a big car. But Paul was wrong again. When he stopped the car, the boy ran into the house and then came back carrying his little crippled brother. He sat him down on the ground and _____8_____ to the car.

"There it is, Buddy, just like I told you. His brother gave it to him and it didn't cost him a cent. And someday I will give you _____9_____ just like it."

Paul got out and lifted the little boy to the front seat of the car. The older brother climbed in beside him and the three of them began a _____10_____ holiday ride.

_____ 1. (A) admitted     (B) agreed     (C) confirmed     (D) nodded

_____ 2. (A) think     (B) speak     (C) mean     (D) tell

_____ 3. (A) hesitated     (B) dominated     (C) nominated     (D) demonstrated

_____ 4. (A) be     (B) have     (C) do     (D) own

_____ 5. (A) watch     (B) saw     (C) read     (D) looked at

_____ 6. (A) like     (B) care     (C) mind     (D) want

_____ 7. (A) ancestors     (B) teachers     (C) enemies     (D) neighbors

_____ 8. (A) pointed     (B) referred     (C) led     (D) showed

_____ 9. (A) that      (B) what      (C) some      (D) one

_____ 10. (A) memorable      (B) memorial      (C) souvenir      (D) remembered

## Part B

    Mahatma Gandhi was India's greatest spiritual and political leader. It was through his effort that India won _____1_____ from Britain. Throughout his life, he _____2_____ his life to peace and brotherhood. Thousands of Indians considered him a _____3_____. They called him Mahatma, _____4_____ "Great Soul."

    Gandhi was born on Oct. 2, 1869 in Porbandar, near Bombay. At 19, he went to study law at University College in London. In 1891, he was _____5_____ to practice law but returned at once to India. Two years later, he went to South Africa, where he saw how his fellow Indians were treated as _____6_____. In 1906, he began his peaceful "revolution."

    Gandhi's methods _____7_____ fasting, peaceful disobedience, and boycotting British goods. Thousands of Indians joined his "civil disobedience." Once in _____8_____ against a salt tax, he led thousands of Indians on a 200-mile march to the sea to make their own salt. His anti-British activities _____9_____ his imprisonment several times. In jail, he would often fast. Fearing that he would _____10_____ to death, the British usually released him quickly. Gandhi's victory came in 1947. Yet less than six months later, he was shot and killed by an assassin.

_____ 1. (A) popularity      (B) resolution      (C) ideals      (D) independence

_____ 2. (A) offered      (B) devoted      (C) selected      (D) discounted

_____ 3. (A) saint      (B) dentist      (C) male      (D) lawyer

_____ 4. (A) means      (B) meant      (C) meaning      (D) to mean

_____ 5. (A) permitted      (B) urged      (C) informed      (D) resisted

_____ 6. (A) superiors      (B) seniors      (C) inferiors      (D) juniors

_____ 7. (A) consisted      (B) constructed      (C) composed      (D) included

_____ 8. (A) protect      (B) prevention      (C) procedure      (D) protest

_____ 9. (A) showed up      (B) led to      (C) resulted from      (D) consisted in

_____ 10. (A) starve      (B) eager      (C) display      (D) deliver

完成日期：_____

智戰語錄

*Learn to walk before you run.*

按部就班。

 實戰演練 Round 2

# I. Vocabulary

_____ 1. Put on your _____. Let's go jogging.

    (A) pajamas     (B) slippers     (C) necktie     (D) sneakers

_____ 2. He is very _____ with the poor. He often donates as much money as possible to charities.

    (A) devoted     (B) determined     (C) generous     (D) willing

_____ 3. After the party, used plates and glasses were _____ around on the table and the floor. It would take hours to clean the mess up.

    (A) laid     (B) lied     (C) lain     (D) lay

_____ 4. The flight attendants standing at the front gate welcomed the passengers _____.

    (A) abroad     (B) broad     (C) aboard     (D) board

_____ 5. A good teacher should be familiar with all kinds of teaching _____.

    (A) calculation     (B) techniques     (C) efficiency     (D) forecast

_____ 6. He didn't give me any _____ that he would quit the job.

    (A) ink     (B) hint     (C) proposal     (D) doubt

_____ 7. It takes constant practice to _____ a skill.

    (A) manufacture     (B) master     (C) marvel     (D) major

_____ 8. She doesn't allow her children to eat the candy because it contains _____ flavors.

    (A) artificial     (B) natural     (C) artistic     (D) ashamed

_____ 9. The students are so excited that they can hardly sit _____.

    (A) still     (B) liberally     (C) deep     (D) tight

_____ 10. How will they escape in case of _____?

    (A) emergency     (B) embarrassment     (C) empire     (D) embassy

_____ 11. There was nothing _____ about the old man's death. He was proved to die of a heart attack.

    (A) miraculous     (B) miserable     (C) marvelous     (D) mysterious

_____ 12. I cannot stand the _____ weather in Alaska.

    (A) fair     (B) warm     (C) bitter     (D) scorching

_____ 13. He is under great _____ because of his new job.

    (A) stress     (B) information     (C) miracle     (D) nonsense

_____ 14. My favorite _____ is sweet and sour chicken.

(A) type      (B) pastime      (C) dish      (D) leftover

_____ 15. The _____ for drunken driving can be several years imprisonment.

     (A) objection      (B) fine      (C) penalty      (D) reward

_____ 16. He is a director known for his serious films but his latest one is a _____ .

     (A) tragedy      (B) comedy      (C) comic      (D) success

_____ 17. Bill did well on his study in high school, so he won a _____ to the university.

     (A) background      (B) determination      (C) scholarship      (D) circulation

_____ 18. At 11:00, the boy _____ went back to his bedroom at his mother's request.

     (A) reluctantly      (B) abruptly      (C) attractively      (D) generously

_____ 19. These guns and bombs are purely _____ weapons, not designed for attack.

     (A) thrilled      (B) permanent      (C) defensive      (D) panic

_____ 20. Does anyone want _____ beef? I just took it from the oven.

     (A) boiled      (B) steamed      (C) roast      (D) fried

## II. Idioms & Phrases

_____ 1. Don't worry. The problem will be solved _____ .

     (A) in vain      (B) for good      (C) sooner or later    (D) off and on

_____ 2. The couple often _____ their children's education.

     (A) compete against    (B) dispute over      (C) end in      (D) count on

_____ 3. He _____ with a knife when his business failed.

     (A) started a new life             (B) took his own life

     (C) managed to survive         (D) lived on his own

_____ 4. When hearing the bad news, she _____ crying.

     (A) burst into      (B) gave forth      (C) let away      (D) burst out

_____ 5. As a student, you have to _____ your time to study.

     (A) make room for            (B) make good use of

     (C) make a difference in      (D) make up for

_____ 6. You have to learn to _____ your fear of the public if you want to be a good speaker.

     (A) get over      (B) get along with      (C) get out      (D) get past

_____ 7. You may borrow the car _____ you promise to keep it in good condition.

     (A) as far as      (B) as well as      (C) as long as      (D) as much as

_____ 8. I believe it's time to _____ the plan _____ .

     (A) stand...to reason    (B) put...into action    (C) leave...along    (D) put...to blame

_____ 9. He is very changeable. He never _____ anything very long.

(A) switches off      (B) sticks to      (C) stirs up      (D) sets aside

_____ 10. More and more people find it hard to _____ right and wrong.

(A) jump at      (B) go on with      (C) get around      (D) distinguish between

## III. Cloze Test

### Part A

A few years ago I read a story about a husband and wife who made a terrible mistake. They had gone shopping and taken their baby ___1___ them. After they had ___2___ their shopping, they returned to their car to go home. When they ___3___ their car, they put the baby in the plastic baby carrier that he rode in for ___4___. The couple then drove off in their car toward home. After they had driven a few miles, they looked in the back ___5___ of the car to see how the baby was. To their ___6___, the baby was not there. The couple drove back to the store but didn't find the baby. They called the police, and they said they had the baby ___7___ it was fine. The baby in the carrier had been put on the ___8___ of the car and fallen to the ground. It was ___9___ by the plastic seat. The ___10___ couple took their baby home and were always careful after that.

_____ 1. (A) along with                    (B) in charge of

   (C) except for                    (D) with reference to

_____ 2. (A) begun        (B) finished        (C) adopted        (D) reduced

_____ 3. (A) adventured   (B) attacked        (C) reached        (D) revenged

_____ 4. (A) collection    (B) destruction     (C) curiosity       (D) safety

_____ 5. (A) trunk        (B) wheel           (C) seat           (D) gear

_____ 6. (A) disappointment (B) sympathy      (C) shock          (D) satisfaction

_____ 7. (A) and          (B) but             (C) who            (D) because

_____ 8. (A) top          (B) tip             (C) toe            (D) tool

_____ 9. (A) destroyed     (B) advised         (C) prevented      (D) protected

_____ 10. (A) honest       (B) greedy          (C) generous       (D) grateful

### Part B

Adult education faces many obstacles. Adults are not accustomed to ___1___ to school and sitting for long hours listening to teachers and reading books. Also, many adults are ___2___ or afraid to go back to school. They often think that they will ___3___ to be stupid or that they will fail. Adults often have little time for education. They have jobs and families and cannot take four or six or eight or more hours every day to go to school. ___4___ these problems, adults often cannot go to school, so school must go to the adults.

Adults have some ___5___ in education, however. Adult learners often know exactly what they need to learn. Because they have the experience of life, they know what ___6___ will be useful to them and what will not. If they cannot read or write, they have experienced the problems that illiteracy can cause. If they cannot do their jobs well, they have experienced the ___7___ of income or of job ___8___ that lack of vocational training can cause. Adults have usually accumulated a wealth of experience of life ___9___ that can help them in learning. They have more ___10___, everyday experience that can help them understand what they learn in school.

_____ 1. (A) leaving     (B) returning     (C) attending     (D) floating

_____ 2. (A) ashamed     (B) excited     (C) astonished     (D) shocked

_____ 3. (A) leap     (B) flutter     (C) appear     (D) observe

_____ 4. (A) Because of     (B) In the middle of     (C) Apart from     (D) At most

_____ 5. (A) examinations     (B) problems     (C) supporters     (D) advantages

_____ 6. (A) necessity     (B) knowledge     (C) hobby     (D) landscape

_____ 7. (A) loss     (B) promotion     (C) increase     (D) value

_____ 8. (A) originalities     (B) inhabitants     (C) locations     (D) opportunities

_____ 9. (A) in jail     (B) in general     (C) by contrast     (D) all at once

_____ 10. (A) worse     (B) stable     (C) practical     (D) normal

完成日期：_____

挑戰語錄

*Least said, soonest mended.*

少說，快改。

## I. Vocabulary

_____ 1. Don't _____ children by giving them too much freedom.

(A) spare      (B) spoil      (C) spin      (D) splash

_____ 2. The artist is _____ with creative talents. His original works impress all those who have been to his exhibition.

(A) illustrated      (B) gifted      (C) imagined      (D) evaluated

_____ 3. In 1989, an Exxon oil tank had an accident in Alaska, and millions of tons of oil was _____ into Prince William Sound.

(A) leaping      (B) leaving      (C) leaking      (D) leading

_____ 4. Your idea is too _____ to understand. Can you give us some concrete examples?

(A) abstract      (B) exact      (C) clear      (D) organized

_____ 5. The farmer put a _____ in his field to frighten birds away.

(A) battery      (B) strawberry      (C) gun      (D) scarecrow

_____ 6. I have some _____ in agreeing to the plan. I fear it may not be practical.

(A) complaint      (B) inspiration      (C) depression      (D) hesitation

_____ 7. The little girl is quite thoughtful and _____ compared to others of her age.

(A) filthy      (B) annoying      (C) mature      (D) foul

_____ 8. She ought to be thoroughly _____ of herself for telling such a lie.

(A) afraid      (B) upset      (C) responsible      (D) ashamed

_____ 9. He got married again _____ after his wife was dead.

(A) highly      (B) shortly      (C) ordinarily      (D) extremely

_____ 10. His first novel succeeded _____ after it was published.

(A) indecisively      (B) inclusively      (C) instantly      (D) instinctively

_____ 11. At the dinner table, you should wipe your mouth with a _____ rather than with your hand.

(A) paper      (B) leaf      (C) stocking      (D) napkin

_____ 12. When I saw such a complicated math problem, my mind went _____.

(A) wrong      (B) blind      (C) blank      (D) deaf

_____ 13. It is a Chinese _____ to eat moon cakes on the Moon Festival.

(A) ceremony      (B) invention      (C) tradition      (D) hesitation

_____ 14. The prisoner heard the verdict without _____. No one knew how he felt about it.

(A) delight        (B) emotion        (C) permission        (D) limit

_____ 15. The rescue _____ has been going quite smoothly. All the passengers and the crew members have been brought back from the sinking ship.

(A) performance        (B) management        (C) operation        (D) technology

_____ 16. Five cowboys worked together to _____ the wild horse.

(A) capture        (B) respond        (C) calculate        (D) free

_____ 17. It is considered impolite to make _____ when eating the soup.

(A) coffee        (B) sounds        (C) commitment        (D) decisions

_____ 18. The local government is too poor to _____ the program.

(A) conquer        (B) invade        (C) finance        (D) download

_____ 19. The _____ of students admitted to college has been increasing these years.

(A) portion        (B) percent        (C) percentage        (D) mount

_____ 20. Louis was a terrible traveling _____—always dirty and complaining.

(A) accent        (B) luggage        (C) companion        (D) airliner

## II. Idioms & Phrases

_____ 1. You can always _____ me when you have trouble.

(A) lead to        (B) account for        (C) compete with        (D) lean on

_____ 2. _____ teaching, she also practices law.

(A) Instead of        (B) Except for        (C) In addition to        (D) As long as

_____ 3. He is late for school again _____.

(A) at most        (B) as usual        (C) for good        (D) at least

_____ 4. Are there enough apples to _____?

(A) go along        (B) go around        (C) go ahead        (D) go away

_____ 5. You must _____ the damage you have caused.

(A) make up for        (B) compensate in        (C) be responsible on        (D) complain about

_____ 6. There are a few parts that I don't like about the movie, but _____ it's an enjoyable film.

(A) by and large        (B) by and by        (C) by the way        (D) in between

_____ 7. Before I made a speech, I was so nervous that I couldn't _____.

(A) stop to tremble        (B) stop trembling        (C) try to trembling        (D) try trembling

_____ 8. Books are being _____ all new students.

(A) distributed to        (B) given off        (C) kept off        (D) aimed at

_____ 9. He _____ to stop himself crying.

(A) bit his lip        (B) ate his words        (C) hit his sacks        (D) blew his horn

_____ 10. If you are going to come to the party, please let me know _____.

(A) soon afterwards    (B) in advance    (C) after all    (D) again and again

## III. Cloze Test

Part A

It has been said that everyone lives by selling something. ____1____ of this statement, teachers live by selling knowledge, ____2____ by selling wisdom and priests by selling ____3____ comfort. Though it may be possible to measure the value of material goods in ____4____ of money, it is extremely difficult to ____5____ the true value of the services people ____6____ for us. There are times when we would willingly give everything we ____7____ to save our lives, yet we might be ____8____ to pay a physician a high fee for offering us ____9____ this service. Skills have to be paid for in ____10____ way that goods are paid for at a shop.

_____ 1. (A) According      (B) In the light    (C) At the sight     (D) For the sake
_____ 2. (A) physicians      (B) psychologists   (C) philosophers     (D) photographers
_____ 3. (A) spiritual       (B) excessive       (C) global           (D) popular
_____ 4. (A) terms           (B) order           (C) agreement        (D) regard
_____ 5. (A) elevate         (B) suspend         (C) estimate         (D) obey
_____ 6. (A) discover        (B) recover         (C) establish        (D) perform
_____ 7. (A) describe        (B) sacrifice       (C) conceal          (D) possess
_____ 8. (A) satisfied       (B) reluctant       (C) astonished       (D) voluntary
_____ 9. (A) precisely       (B) completely      (C) fortunately      (D) partly
_____ 10. (A) the other      (B) another         (C) the same         (D) some other

Part B

Loans are an important banking service. A bank can give money to businesses and to individual people. The bank may loan money to a business to buy more machines or ____1____. For example, a bakery may borrow money from the bank to buy more ____2____. The bank may also ____3____ money to individuals. Some people borrow money from the bank to build swimming pools or to ____4____ their houses. The bank always charges interest on loans. The borrower must repay the loan ____5____ the interest.

_____ 1. (A) gowns        (B) tools        (C) employers    (D) novels
_____ 2. (A) ovens        (B) bread        (C) pigeons      (D) telescopes
_____ 3. (A) distribute   (B) download     (C) examine      (D) isolate
_____ 4. (A) react        (B) recite       (C) regulate     (D) repair
_____ 5. (A) regardless   (B) exceeding    (C) plus         (D) through

( Part C )

Britain is an ___1___, of course, and you are never far from the sea. Some parts of the ___2___, especially in the west, are wild and rocky, with small, sandy beaches, and romantic ___3___. Other parts are ___4___. The east coast of Scotland, for example, is busy with oil rigs and fishing boats. The most popular beaches are near the many ___5___ towns on the south coast, where the weather is usually warmer. It is here that Londoners come to relax.

_____ 1. (A) organization    (B) island    (C) industry    (D) expert
_____ 2. (A) mountain    (B) county    (C) cliff    (D) coast
_____ 3. (A) harbors    (B) candles    (C) legends    (D) intentions
_____ 4. (A) peaceful    (B) joyful    (C) industrial    (D) intense
_____ 5. (A) holiday    (B) greedy    (C) grateful    (D) empty

完成日期：_____

**震戰語錄**

*A miss is as good as a mile.*

失之毫釐，差之千里。

## I. Vocabulary

_____ 1. The Central Mountains _____ for hundreds of kilometers from north to south.

(A) prevents     (B) reacts     (C) stretches     (D) counts

_____ 2. There is no _____ for success. Success belongs to those who work hard.

(A) way     (B) formula     (C) depression     (D) reason

_____ 3. Many weight-conscious housewives have used _____ meat instead of regular meat in their meals.

(A) thin     (B) lean     (C) slim     (D) slender

_____ 4. The TV show is a(n) _____ reflection of life and relationship in New York.

(A) accurate     (B) intimate     (C) official     (D) stubborn

_____ 5. What the newspaper said is not always a fair _____ of what really happened.

(A) instrument     (B) statement     (C) movement     (D) sportsmanship

_____ 6. To my _____, my close friend was a killer of ten innocent children.

(A) regret     (B) entertainment     (C) horror     (D) amusement

_____ 7. The taxi can take a _____ of four passengers. Now that there are six of us, we need two taxis.

(A) majority     (B) minority     (C) maximum     (D) minimum

_____ 8. Maggie has _____ a fascinating doll's house.

(A) assisted     (B) assembled     (C) beat     (D) dined

_____ 9. I don't like to take part in _____ activities. I am not used to facing strangers.

(A) facial     (B) social     (C) creative     (D) artificial

_____ 10. I live within my _____. I only get things I can afford.

(A) evaluation     (B) ranking     (C) rate     (D) income

_____ 11. You shouldn't have made such _____ remarks about Brian. After all, he is your brother.

(A) educational     (B) generous     (C) holy     (D) nasty

_____ 12. He cut his finger and lost a lot of _____.

(A) muscle     (B) liquor     (C) stream     (D) blood

_____ 13. She _____ the room with her sister. She longed for her own room.

(A) shared     (B) occupied     (C) flashed     (D) displayed

_____ 14. My English teacher lays as much _____ on written work as on oral practice.

(A) intonation     (B) emphasis     (C) guidance     (D) instruction

_____ 15. There will be a big sale in the department store next week. I won't miss the
_____ to pick up a few good bargains.

    (A) advantage     (B) opportunity     (C) benefit     (D) registration

_____ 16. Many tourists _____ their names on the tree.

    (A) erased     (B) carved     (C) risked     (D) arranged

_____ 17. She felt _____ for the homeless children, and donated some money to help
them.

    (A) proud     (B) sympathy     (C) defensive     (D) delighted

_____ 18. He was heavily _____ for speeding.

    (A) fined     (B) defeated     (C) paid     (D) passed

_____ 19. This is private property. You cannot enter without _____.

    (A) impression     (B) description     (C) permission     (D) procession

_____ 20. The two athletes are _____ for the gold medal.

    (A) competing     (B) completing     (C) composing     (D) computing

## II. Idioms & Phrases

_____ 1. Our efforts were _____ and the method didn't work.

    (A) by heart     (B) inside out     (C) in vain     (D) once in a while

_____ 2. You had better _____ your father's advice. He has more experience than you.

    (A) thank to     (B) call for     (C) go by     (D) check in

_____ 3. Some people _____ to stay in perfect shape.

    (A) make out     (B) line up     (C) exert influence     (D) go to great lengths

_____ 4. Once you know how to swim, diving is _____.

    (A) a cup of tea     (B) as busy as a bee     (C) a piece of cake     (D) as blind as a bat

_____ 5. Let's go to the _____ and get something to eat.

    (A) stand guard     (B) fair play     (C) snack bar     (D) hot pot

_____ 6. He is _____ a list of the guests for the lunch.

    (A) operating on     (B) picking up     (C) pulling out     (D) drawing up

_____ 7. The singer did surprisingly well in her latest album. _____ a hundred thousand
CD's were sold in the first month when it was released.

    (A) No more than     (B) No less than     (C) Less than     (D) None other than

_____ 8. You should _____ this week's low prices and buy more.

    (A) take advantage of     (B) do your best     (C) take charge of     (D) put into practice

_____ 9. Such a lazy man as Tom _____ fail.

    (A) is able to     (B) is sure to     (C) is suited to     (D) is known to

_____ 10. I don't _____ golf. I find it boring.

    (A) leave for     (B) go in for     (C) have nothing on (D) make up for

## III. Cloze Test

    Living things often depend on each other to ___1___. In some places, such as the oceans and the tropical ___2___, thousands of species may be living together ___3___. These living creatures also ___4___ with the nonliving things around them. Such areas of close interdependence in nature are ___5___ ecosystems. These ecosystems, however, do more than support the ___6___ and animals that live in them. They also influence the ___7___ of the entire planet. The ecosystems of tropical rain forests, ___8___, protect the entire planet by returning water to the ___9___ as vapor and by providing much of the oxygen that we ___10___. One of the ___11___ of these is the rain forest of the Amazon River Basin in Brazil. This forest is ___12___ as large as the United States. It protects many ___13___ species, and it ___14___ controlling the earth's atmosphere and ___15___. However, it is being ___16___ to provide farm land. Little is being done to ___17___ this destruction. Many people do not ___18___ to understand that the failure to ___19___ the Amazon rain forest could have serious ___20___ for all living things.

_____ 1. (A) declare     (B) dread     (C) survive     (D) predict

_____ 2. (A) sprays     (B) mines     (C) rockets     (D) forests

_____ 3. (A) in this way     (B) in no way     (C) by the way     (D) on the way

_____ 4. (A) interact     (B) interchange     (C) interpret     (D) interrupt

_____ 5. (A) known to     (B) known as     (C) famous for     (D) popular with

_____ 6. (A) squares     (B) puzzles     (C) plants     (D) politics

_____ 7. (A) environment     (B) parrot     (C) subject     (D) tourism

_____ 8. (A) that is     (B) in a word     (C) at best     (D) for example

_____ 9. (A) gas     (B) air     (C) metal     (D) pool

_____ 10. (A) witness     (B) breathe     (C) exceed     (D) instruct

_____ 11. (A) largest     (B) great     (C) most     (D) least

_____ 12. (A) eventually     (B) mentally     (C) almost     (D) loosely

_____ 13. (A) medical     (B) furious     (C) hesitant     (D) unique

_____ 14. (A) plays a major role in     (B) takes the place of

    (C) gets rid of     (D) loses sight of

_____ 15. (A) audience     (B) weather     (C) colony     (D) march

_____ 16. (A) lit     (B) grasped     (C) destroyed     (D) irritated

_____ 17. (A) invent     (B) manufacture     (C) prevent     (D) persuade

| | | | |
|---|---|---|---|
| _____ 18. (A) remain | (B) seem | (C) threaten | (D) wander |
| _____ 19. (A) preserve | (B) deserve | (C) serve | (D) reserve |
| _____ 20. (A) causes | (B) factors | (C) reasons | (D) consequences |

完成日期：_____

*Hitch your wagon to a star.*

志在千里。

## I. Vocabulary

_____ 1. The patient is receiving new _____ for lung cancer.

    (A) treatment      (B) chart      (C) bandage      (D) admission

_____ 2. I think this candidate best _____ our requirements. Therefore, I will vote for him.

    (A) fulfills      (B) applies      (C) answers      (D) rejects

_____ 3. Mr. Spencer is going to give a _____ on business management next week.

    (A) lettuce      (B) lecture      (C) fracture      (D) miniature

_____ 4. I have a lot of business _____ but very few real friends.

    (A) companions      (B) ministers      (C) immigrants      (D) acquaintances

_____ 5. His house is _____ by trees. Everything you see from the window is green, green, and green.

    (A) threatened      (B) impressed      (C) surrounded      (D) astonished

_____ 6. More and more people choose to go to this _____ course.

    (A) basketball      (B) tennis      (C) golf      (D) skating

_____ 7. He used a folding ruler to _____ the room before he laid a carpet in it.

    (A) lengthen      (B) count      (C) research      (D) measure

_____ 8. The _____ in the restaurant is so romantic that many people like to eat there.

    (A) atmosphere      (B) reservation      (C) waiters      (D) check

_____ 9. The refugees are badly in need of _____. They lack clothing and food.

    (A) surprise      (B) sunrise      (C) supplies      (D) surgery

_____ 10. There is every _____ that the patient will recover soon.

    (A) independence      (B) individual      (C) indication      (D) inclusion

_____ 11. At the International Conference, you can meet students of different _____.

    (A) counties      (B) nationalities      (C) identities      (D) humanities

_____ 12. The music of the piano _____ sweetly with her voice.

    (A) blended      (B) divided      (C) hid      (D) varied

_____ 13. She is my best friend. I share my _____ and happiness with her.

    (A) pillow      (B) hollow      (C) sorrow      (D) willow

_____ 14. I don't think you can justify the _____ of capital punishment. I prefer it to be abolished.

    (A) removal      (B) employment      (C) campaign      (D) dismissal

_____ 15. You have the right to assert your opinions, but at the same time, you should listen to the _____ point of view.

(A) opposite      (B) various      (C) numerous      (D) additional

_____ 16. For some people, _____ clothes means a T-shirt and jeans.

(A) casual      (B) occupied      (C) fit      (D) cotton

_____ 17. Your roommate is such an ill-mannered fellow. How can you _____ his rudeness?

(A) express      (B) demonstrate      (C) tolerate      (D) exchange

_____ 18. The airplane burst into _____ and all the passengers were killed.

(A) sight      (B) flames      (C) tears      (D) laughter

_____ 19. The son is trying to _____ his father to lend him the car.

(A) persuade      (B) demand      (C) inquire      (D) influence

_____ 20. The rules are a bit too _____ to follow. No wonder many people violate them.

(A) simple      (B) reluctant      (C) complicated      (D) previous

## II. Idioms & Phrases

_____ 1. He is afraid that if he fails, he may _____ his parents _____.

(A) lead...to      (B) take...in      (C) let...down      (D) drop...off

_____ 2. I think your plan _____ being improved a lot.

(A) is able to      (B) is about to      (C) is a bit of      (D) is capable of

_____ 3. I introduced them and then they _____ with each other.

(A) got upset      (B) shook hands      (C) broke up      (D) made up

_____ 4. I don't know what to _____ such a large sum of money.

(A) go with      (B) do with      (C) go through      (D) do away

_____ 5. He got hit in the head and was _____.

(A) knocked up      (B) knocked over      (C) knocked about      (D) knocked out

_____ 6. The concert was _____ the relief of the 921 earthquake.

(A) in care of      (B) benefited from      (C) in aid of      (D) afraid of

_____ 7. I drove to the gas station because I almost _____ gas.

(A) was filled with      (B) ran out of      (C) ended up with      (D) was based on

_____ 8. There is no need to _____ details now. What I need is the general idea.

(A) go into      (B) go without      (C) go around      (D) go near to

_____ 9. We will do everything we can to _____ the standard set by the teacher.

(A) live up to      (B) live on      (C) make up with      (D) make believe

_____ 10. Who is going to _____ Grandma when I'm on the business trip?

(A) take after          (B) look over          (C) take care of          (D) put aside

## III. Cloze Test

### Part A

Protecting the environment is important to me. Like everyone else, I have a ____1____ to leave our Earth in a condition at ____2____ as good as I found it. It is our duty to leave our ____3____ a healthy planet. I believe we should all be like those ____4____ Americans whose religion required them to consider how their actions would affect the coming generations. One small contribution I can make is to ____5____ the size of my family so as not to contribute to the exploding ____6____ growth that threatens the environment and the quality of life for everyone. I can also vote for those ____7____ candidates who can look further into the future than the ____8____ election.

No one wants to live in ____9____. However, it is not necessary for us to be rich in order to be happy, for our education has ____10____ us to lead a full life.

| | | | | |
|---|---|---|---|---|
| _____ 1. (A) responsibility | (B) compromise | (C) tendency | (D) temptation |
| _____ 2. (A) most | (B) least | (C) best | (D) first |
| _____ 3. (A) graduates | (B) ancestors | (C) guides | (D) grandchildren |
| _____ 4. (A) Natural | (B) Primitive | (C) Native | (D) Modern |
| _____ 5. (A) increase | (B) multiply | (C) limit | (D) maximize |
| _____ 6. (A) pollution | (B) traffic | (C) food | (D) population |
| _____ 7. (A) political | (B) job | (C) business | (D) illegal |
| _____ 8. (A) past | (B) next | (C) last | (D) latest |
| _____ 9. (A) wealth | (B) luxury | (C) poverty | (D) ease |
| _____ 10. (A) prepared | (B) prohibited | (C) prevented | (D) preserved |

### Part B

How does television affect our lives? It can be very helpful to people who carefully choose the shows that they watch. Moreover, it benefits elderly people who can't often ____1____ the house, as well as ____2____ in hospitals. It also offers nonnative speakers the advantage of daily informal ____3____ practice; they can increase their vocabulary and ____4____ listening.

On the other hand, there are several serious disadvantages to television. Recent studies show that after only thirty seconds of TV, a person's brain ____5____ the same way it does just after the person falls asleep. Another effect of television on the human brain is that it seems to cause ____6____ concentration. In addition, TV often causes people to become dissatisfied with their own lives. To them, TV becomes more real than ____7____, and their own lives seems

boring. Also, many people get upset when they can't solve problems in real life as ___8___ as
TV actors seem to. The most ___9___ effect of TV might be people's addiction to it. People
often feel a strange and ___10___ need to watch TV even when they don't enjoy it.

| | | | |
|---|---|---|---|
| _____ 1. (A) clean | (B) move | (C) leave | (D) fix |
| _____ 2. (A) doctors | (B) nurses | (C) social workers | (D) patients |
| _____ 3. (A) language | (B) writing | (C) mechanical | (D) imaginary |
| _____ 4. (A) avoid | (B) enjoy | (C) finish | (D) practice |
| _____ 5. (A) releases | (B) relaxes | (C) relieves | (D) revives |
| _____ 6. (A) poor | (B) better | (C) intense | (D) absolute |
| _____ 7. (A) performance | (B) play | (C) reality | (D) concrete |
| _____ 8. (A) good | (B) quickly | (C) easy | (D) hardly |
| _____ 9. (A) beneficial | (B) positive | (C) passive | (D) negative |
| _____ 10. (A) enthusiastic | (B) powerful | (C) wonderful | (D) reasonable |

完成日期：_____

## 實戰語錄

*A still tongue makes a wise head.*
舌少動則腦精明。

# I. Vocabulary

_____ 1. The bad news came as a great _____ to me. I cannot believe it at all.

(A) accomplishment　(B) circumstance　(C) demonstration　(D) shock

_____ 2. I _____ whenever my teacher asks me to answer her question. My silence always makes her fly into a temper.

(A) scare　　　(B) frighten　　(C) discourage　(D) freeze

_____ 3. If the man still refuses to return the money, we are going to take _____ actions against him.

(A) gentle　　　(B) legal　　　(C) mental　　　(D) fatal

_____ 4. His son _____ some very unpleasant habits when he was in high school.

(A) acquired　　(B) required　　(C) realized　　(D) entered

_____ 5. Li Po, who wrote many great poems, was a poet _____ of the name.

(A) worthy　　　(B) jealous　　(C) fond　　　(D) considerate

_____ 6. He was _____ born. His parents were low in their social status.

(A) humbly　　　(B) lightly　　(C) heavily　　(D) gratefully

_____ 7. I have difficulty _____ all my friends' phone numbers, so I have to keep them in a notebook.

(A) recording　　(B) managing　(C) memorizing　(D) contacting

_____ 8. He _____ his photo to this application form.

(A) assured　　　(B) collected　(C) attached　　(D) gained

_____ 9. Many animals and insects _____ food for winter.

(A) stores　　　(B) stirs　　　(C) strikes　　(D) struggles

_____ 10. _____ told her to lie still and pretend to be dead.

(A) Instinct　　(B) Stick　　　(C) Extinct　　(D) Distinct

_____ 11. She speaks French so fluently that she sounds exactly like a _____ speaker.

(A) native　　　(B) national　(C) local　　　(D) country

_____ 12. There's something in your eye—try _____ your eyes a few times.

(A) covering　　(B) blinking　(C) closed　　(D) open

_____ 13. Red color may be a _____ of danger.

(A) harvest　　　(B) dose　　　(C) symbol　　(D) fantasy

_____ 14. We have to do something to keep _____ species from dying out.

(A) evolved　　　(B) endangered　(C) poisoned　(D) enormous

_____ 15. Before she went into the show business and became a star, she had been regarded as only a(n) _____ girl in her hometown.

(A) unique      (B) talented      (C) ideal      (D) ordinary

_____ 16. I bought some new dresses through a mail-order _____.

(A) products      (B) catalogue      (C) dialogue      (D) cooperation

_____ 17. The _____ of his election campaign is "Trust me with your future."

(A) eraser      (B) fiction      (C) slogan      (D) headline

_____ 18. He gave me a _____ refusal, which made me feel discouraged.

(A) fat      (B) flat      (C) fate      (D) fled

_____ 19. I am not used to _____ contact with strangers. Even a handshake makes me uneasy.

(A) mental      (B) physical      (C) spiritual      (D) psychological

_____ 20. When he called me a workaholic, I took it as a _____.

(A) completion      (B) composition      (C) concert      (D) compliment

## II. Idioms & Phrases

_____ 1. Her misbehavior _____ her family.

(A) made a difference in      (B) brought shame on

(C) let go of      (D) got used to

_____ 2. Times are hard and we have to _____ any luxury.

(A) do with      (B) do away with      (C) cut in      (D) stick to

_____ 3. The secret of success _____ diligence and perseverance.

(A) lives in      (B) lies in      (C) comes in      (D) consists of

_____ 4. I hate traveling _____ because I get horribly airsick.

(A) in the air      (B) on the air      (C) off the air      (D) by air

_____ 5. The twins look so much alike that I cannot _____ one _____ the other.

(A) prevent...from      (B) stop...from      (C) tell...from      (D) protect...from

_____ 6. To my disappointment, he didn't _____ his promise.

(A) look into      (B) make good      (C) take after      (D) make out

_____ 7. The flight from Taipei to New York City takes sixteen hours _____.

(A) or so      (B) by and large      (C) so so      (D) as much

_____ 8. Will miniskirts _____ as the most fashionable clothes again?

(A) catch up      (B) catch on      (C) turn up      (D) live on

_____ 9. To attract the attention of children, the baker made the cookies _____ of stars.

(A) in any sense      (B) by means of      (C) in the shape      (D) for a moment

_____ 10. The wealthy woman has been _____ five husbands.

(A) divided into    (B) divorced from    (C) engaged in    (D) driven away

## III. Cloze Test

Part A

Very early on, when he was eight, Steven Spielberg was drawn to filmmaking, although he had seen few movies. He ___1___ being fascinated by visual images. ___2___ his obsession with the visual came a(n) ___3___ for storytelling. He loved telling stories because he wanted to be the ___4___ of attention. He came from a family of three younger sisters, and they were fighting for their ___5___ in the family. Spielberg did something ___6___: he had a movie camera and he could make movies. It was how he found his position in the family. He knew this was going to be a(n) ___7___, not just a hobby. He had learned that film was ___8___. In his late teens, Spielberg moved with his family to California, where he attended high school and continued making his movies. He ___9___ his academic studies, and his grades reflected it. As a result, after graduation, he wasn't ___10___ by any major film school. Finally he attended Cal State at Long Beach. During this period, he made a 22-minute short, *Amblin'*. This small movie changed his life.

_____ 1. (A) reminded    (B) recalled    (C) occurred    (D) memorized
_____ 2. (A) Out of    (B) Up to    (C) Away from    (D) Down under
_____ 3. (A) action    (B) ability    (C) present    (D) gift
_____ 4. (A) middle    (B) medium    (C) heart    (D) center
_____ 5. (A) position    (B) condition    (C) division    (D) nutrition
_____ 6. (A) queer    (B) peculiar    (C) unique    (D) individual
_____ 7. (A) interest    (B) knowledge    (C) career    (D) occupation
_____ 8. (A) power    (B) fad    (C) fantasy    (D) wealth
_____ 9. (A) stressed    (B) stopped    (C) intensified    (D) neglected
_____ 10. (A) reacted    (B) accepted    (C) responded    (D) replied

Part B

The ___1___ of UFOs (Unidentified Flying Objects) is a source of controversy that often ___2___ people into two separate groups: those who believe that UFOs are the spaceships of intelligent ___3___ from other planets, and those who ___4___ and believe these sightings have some other explanation. Those in the second group say these sightings could be ___5___ the effects of a distant planet, a weather ___6___, or airplane lights, for example. Another possible explanation is that the people who report the sightings could be imagining what they

saw or _____7_____ stories to draw attention. Are these people trying to _____8_____ us? Are they confused and possibly showing signs of _____9_____ problems? Or are some of them telling the _____10_____?

_____ 1. (A) mission       (B) conference       (C) existence       (D) passion

_____ 2. (A) inspires       (B) leans       (C) inserts       (D) divides

_____ 3. (A) ministers       (B) psychologists       (C) viruses       (D) beings

_____ 4. (A) inject       (B) switch       (C) disagree       (D) recite

_____ 5. (A) as a result of       (B) due to       (C) supposed to       (D) based on

_____ 6. (A) disturbance       (B) volunteer       (C) vision       (D) supervisor

_____ 7. (A) hanging on       (B) looking up       (C) making up       (D) settling down

_____ 8. (A) have a way with       (B) have it out with       (C) play tricks on       (D) call attention to

_____ 9. (A) physical       (B) financial       (C) critical       (D) mental

_____ 10. (A) truth       (B) fiction       (C) lie       (D) literature

完成日期：＿＿＿＿＿＿＿＿

實戰語錄

*A mill cannot grind with the water that is past.*

往者不可諫，來者猶可追。

## I. Vocabulary

_____ 1. With a wave of a stick, the magician made the rabbit _____.

    (A) visit     (B) value     (C) vanish     (D) view

_____ 2. The hospital was _____ in 1920. It has served patients for more than eighty years.

    (A) founded     (B) found     (C) fined     (D) fanned

_____ 3. His miraculous survival after the plane crash has become a _____. It is still remembered and talked about even ten years afterwards.

    (A) romance     (B) tradition     (C) legend     (D) rumor

_____ 4. I got bad grades because I didn't have _____ time to prepare.

    (A) obvious     (B) effective     (C) adequate     (D) limited

_____ 5. The country is in a dangerous _____ because one general of the army intends to overthrow the government.

    (A) significance     (B) situation     (C) signature     (D) sincerity

_____ 6. He likes singing. He is always _____ while he is working.

    (A) hugging     (B) hammering     (C) humming     (D) hushing

_____ 7. It was a great honor for him that the president made special _____ of his name in the speech.

    (A) mention     (B) certain     (C) use     (D) effort

_____ 8. None of our _____ to contact Jimmy was successful.

    (A) attempts     (B) trials     (C) notices     (D) warnings

_____ 9. Buses or trains are my means of _____ to school.

    (A) transportation     (B) observation     (C) digestion     (D) demonstration

_____ 10. The street is _____-packed with cars.

    (A) jewel     (B) jelly     (C) jaw     (D) jam

_____ 11. I am _____, so I cannot drive without wearing my glasses.

    (A) short-handed     (B) narrow-minded     (C) near-sighted     (D) forward-looking

_____ 12. The young boy _____ when talking to a beautiful girl.

    (A) cried     (B) blushed     (C) knelt     (D) jumped

_____ 13. He is so _____ that it is impossible for him to change his mind.

    (A) flexible     (B) energetic     (C) diligent     (D) stubborn

_____ 14. We all wish for _____ peace in the world. No country would fight against

another.

    (A) during        (B) enduring        (C) internal        (D) domestic

_____ 15. If the fruit is grown _____, that means the farmers do not use chemicals on it.

    (A) organically     (B) biologically     (C) economically     (D) effectively

_____ 16. To avoid pollution, we must _____ dumping trash into the sea.

    (A) permit        (B) protect        (C) practice        (D) cease

_____ 17. The water is boiling and you can see _____ out of the kettle.

    (A) stereo        (B) stream        (C) steam        (D) steak

_____ 18. She is a _____ person. She can adapt to new situations easily.

    (A) flexible        (B) spoiled        (C) graceful        (D) stubborn

_____ 19. The _____ gave me a check-up and told me everything was fine.

    (A) physician     (B) philosopher     (C) physicist     (D) psychologist

_____ 20. Do you believe in the _____ of global village?

    (A) concern        (B) concept        (C) pressure        (D) analysis

## II. Idioms & Phrases

_____ 1. You must _____ for the passing cars when you cross the streets.

    (A) look up        (B) look down        (C) look in        (D) look out

_____ 2. They can't afford daily necessities, _____ luxuries.

    (A) let alone     (B) with regard to     (C) in support of     (D) in shortage of

_____ 3. _____ your comic book _____ and do your homework.

    (A) Demand...of     (B) Keep...in mind     (C) Ask...out     (D) Set...aside

_____ 4. This agreement _____ for a year.

    (A) holds good     (B) stands still     (C) lies open     (D) breaks loose

_____ 5. Even though they were lost in the forest, they didn't _____ and managed to find a way out.

    (A) hang around     (B) lose their head     (C) poke their heads     (D) count heads

_____ 6. Even though you've been there before, bring a map just _____.

    (A) in case        (B) in addition        (C) in no case        (D) in case of

_____ 7. We _____ the heavy rain in the doorway.

    (A) took our turns                 (B) took place

    (C) took shelter from            (D) took advantage of

_____ 8. The old man has experienced _____ of life.

    (A) to and fro     (B) ups and downs     (C) back and forth     (D) in and out

_____ 9. His family is very poor, and it is _____ that they can provide any financial help

for him to go to college.

(A) out of question          (B) in question

(C) beyond question        (D) out of the question

_____ 10. Max was transferred to the branch in Paris _____ three other engineers.

(A) taken altogether    (B) along with      (C) with an aid of     (D) above all

## III. Cloze Test

### Part A

In the U.S., even people can be in fashion or out of date. In 1987, for example, an exterminator in Texas decided that he needed more people to pay him to kill the ___1___ in their houses. He had a ___2___ idea of an advertisement in a local newspaper: he ___3___ to pay $1,000 to the person who could find the biggest cockroach. This ___4___ offer made him suddenly famous. There were stories about him nationwide. ___5___, this kind of fame does not ___6___ long. Such people are famous for a short ___7___ of time. This is the ___8___ of a fad: it comes and goes very fast. A person who ___9___ fads should remember that they may come back in ___10___ after 10 to 15 years of being "out." So it might be a good idea never to throw anything away.

_____ 1. (A) pats          (B) passes         (C) pets          (D) pests

_____ 2. (A) novel        (B) fictitious     (C) realistic     (D) fashionable

_____ 3. (A) afforded     (B) provided    (C) offered      (D) supported

_____ 4. (A) plain        (B) modest      (C) false        (D) queer

_____ 5. (A) Otherwise    (B) Besides     (C) Consequently    (D) However

_____ 6. (A) remain      (B) leave       (C) last         (D) maintain

_____ 7. (A) period      (B) piece       (C) part        (D) moment

_____ 8. (A) trend       (B) factor      (C) principal    (D) essence

_____ 9. (A) takes place   (B) participates in   (C) participates   (D) takes place in

_____ 10. (A) type        (B) date        (C) form        (D) style

### Part B

Eating is not easy aboard the spacecraft. If you ___1___ coffee or juice, it just floats around the ___2___ in balls. Salt is impossible to use in space. The ___3___ of salt won't come out of the salt shaker. ___4___, you have to use salt and pepper in liquid ___5___. Astronauts now know that they must not take chili into space. On one flight, containers of food with chili ___6___ when the astronauts opened them. Before the flight, all food must be precooked, dehydrated, and ___7___. To return ___8___ to the food, you have to use a

__9__ to put water into the packages. Foods like peanut butter, puddings, or sauces are the easiest to eat because they ____10____ to your spoon. Other food just floats off your spoon.

_____ 1. (A) spell      (B) heat      (C) drift      (D) spill

_____ 2. (A) dock      (B) deck      (C) cabin      (D) limb

_____ 3. (A) grains      (B) piles      (C) models      (D) petals

_____ 4. (A) Instead      (B) Therefore      (C) However      (D) Nevertheless

_____ 5. (A) district      (B) form      (C) dynasty      (D) embassy

_____ 6. (A) eliminated      (B) flunked      (C) inspected      (D) exploded

_____ 7. (A) boiled      (B) frozen      (C) packaged      (D) roasted

_____ 8. (A) muscle      (B) pasta      (C) moisture      (D) passage

_____ 9. (A) needle      (B) glue      (C) scissor      (D) knife

_____ 10. (A) fasten      (B) stick      (C) belong      (D) refer

完成日期：_____

*More haste, less speed.*
欲速則不達。

## I. Vocabulary

_____ 1. He is a man of great _____. He can lift up a motorcycle.

(A) development     (B) strength     (C) faith     (D) evidence

_____ 2. The little boy attended his mother's _____ service, not knowing why she was lying still in a wooden box.

(A) wedding     (B) charity     (C) church     (D) funeral

_____ 3. After a tiring day, it is relaxing to take a _____ walk along the beach.

(A) hastily     (B) specifically     (C) hesitantly     (D) leisurely

_____ 4. The political party has tended to _____ more moderate policies these years.

(A) adapt     (B) adjust     (C) adopt     (D) advise

_____ 5. She felt _____ and yawned.

(A) slippery     (B) friendly     (C) sleepy     (D) lousy

_____ 6. The whole _____ chores are done by the mother.

(A) houses     (B) household     (C) housewife     (D) housekeeper

_____ 7. The prisoner of war begged his enemy for _____ to spare his life.

(A) acceptance     (B) support     (C) assistance     (D) mercy

_____ 8. She takes the _____ that children should learn at their own pace.

(A) proposal     (B) project     (C) preference     (D) attitude

_____ 9. She shrugged her _____ and said she had no idea.

(A) fists     (B) wrinkles     (C) ankles     (D) shoulders

_____ 10. Every summer London is _____ by tourists.

(A) invaded     (B) prayed     (C) restored     (D) investigated

_____ 11. The cell phone is no longer a fancy modern device. It has become a _____ to many people. They cannot do without it.

(A) fad     (B) luxury     (C) necessity     (D) benefit

_____ 12. Most parents enjoy _____ about their children's achievements.

(A) complaining     (B) teasing     (C) boasting     (D) reporting

_____ 13. She is my best friend. I will always _____ our friendship.

(A) determine     (B) cease     (C) waste     (D) treasure

_____ 14. Strict discipline is _____ on all students. No one can avoid it.

(A) forced     (B) afforded     (C) enforced     (D) provided

_____ 15. The United Nations is an _____ meant to promote international cooperation and

world peace.

(A) accommodation  (B) organization  (C) abbreviation  (D) information

_____ 16. His cell phone is only 8 _____ long.

(A) meters        (B) millimeters    (C) centimeters    (D) feet

_____ 17. All the _____ and field events are going to be very competitive in the game.

(A) track         (B) distance      (C) direction     (D) weight

_____ 18. She is always fooled by his _____ . It's foolish of her to believe his insincere praise to be true.

(A) respect      (B) philosophy    (C) flattery     (D) resignation

_____ 19. Many people do not realize that _____ videos or music is a crime.

(A) playing     (B) collecting    (C) pirating     (D) recording

_____ 20. I'd like to _____ a reservation for a single room on August 12<sup>th</sup>.

(A) confess     (B) confirm     (C) conclude    (D) commute

## II. Idioms & Phrases

_____ 1. Please _____ the volume of the TV set. I have to study now.

(A) turn down   (B) turn up    (C) turn in    (D) turn over

_____ 2. The ferryboat was _____ by a dense fog.

(A) raised up   (B) let up     (C) caught up   (D) held up

_____ 3. No matter how hard he tried to explain, I still couldn't _____ the whole situation.

(A) hook up    (B) imagine as   (C) get the picture of  (D) reach out

_____ 4. Put the vase _____ of the table so that it won't be knocked off.

(A) at the bottom  (B) at the margin  (C) on the top   (D) in the center

_____ 5. _____ , postmen send letters regularly every day.

(A) Up and down  (B) Odds and ends  (C) Over and over  (D) Rain or shine

_____ 6. All my time and effort went _____ and I had to start all over again.

(A) down the drain         (B) to extremes

(C) on and on            (D) back on my words

_____ 7. The place had changed so much that we got _____ and couldn't find our way.

(A) mixed up   (B) lined up    (C) mapped out  (D) passed out

_____ 8. The victims of the flood has _____ twenty.

(A) dropped off  (B) amounted to  (C) put on     (D) adjusted to

_____ 9. The husband _____ his wife _____ and never came back to her again.

(A) took...for granted  (B) left...behind   (C) took...apart   (D) saw...off

_____ 10. _____ a minute please. He's on the other line right now.

    (A) Talk over      (B) Keep off      (C) Get hold of      (D) Hold on

# III. Cloze Test

### Part A

After I graduated from medical college, I began to _____1_____ medicine in my hometown. My office is about two miles from our old house. Some of my _____2_____ are people who have known me for a long time. And my mom and dad stop by _____3_____. My parents come to the office for _____4_____ visits and lab tests. They also come at _____5_____ times, like when they are shopping at the _____6_____ or just passing by. The _____7_____ and receptionists are _____8_____ used to seeing them. They just wave as my parents _____9_____ through the lobby on their way back to my office or exam rooms. Sometimes a new employee will give them a worried look, but they soon learn to _____10_____ the smiling woman with the gray hair and the man with the accent.

_____ 1. (A) experiment     (B) major       (C) practice      (D) instruct

_____ 2. (A) customers      (B) clients       (C) guests       (D) patients

_____ 3. (A) once and for all          (B) once in a while

          (C) once upon a time         (D) once in a lifetime

_____ 4. (A) route        (B) routine      (C) rough       (D) roundabout

_____ 5. (A) other        (B) another      (C) the other      (D) others

_____ 6. (A) hall          (B) fall         (C) call         (D) mall

_____ 7. (A) officials       (B) managers     (C) clerks       (D) nurses

_____ 8. (A) pretty        (B) prettily      (C) hard        (D) hardly

_____ 9. (A) past         (B) pass        (C) passed      (D) paste

_____ 10. (A) understand     (B) acquaint     (C) acquire      (D) recognize

### Part B

Today, triathlons are much more popular _____1_____ ordinary athletes. People of all _____2_____ —from teens to seventies—can compete _____3_____ they are in good physical _____4_____. In fact, it has become a great family sport, with fathers and mothers training with their sons and daughters. Triathletes are special people who have time in their lives for _____5_____ and families. Most are highly _____6_____ and earn top salaries in their jobs. They are people who are very _____7_____. Many triathletes are happily _____8_____. In fact, two-thirds of triathletes say that their training has _____9_____ influence on their marriages. Today, the triathlon is an Olympic sport and a respected event _____10_____.

_____ 1. (A) inside        (B) among      (C) through      (D) minus

|   |   |   |   |   |
|---|---|---|---|---|
| _____ | 2. (A) classes | (B) types | (C) religions | (D) ages |
| _____ | 3. (A) as long as | (B) no sooner | (C) what if | (D) but that |
| _____ | 4. (A) status | (B) level | (C) condition | (D) construction |
| _____ | 5. (A) enthusiasm | (B) exhibitions | (C) careers | (D) future |
| _____ | 6. (A) respected | (B) recommended | (C) seized | (D) educated |
| _____ | 7. (A) competitive | (B) severe | (C) tremendous | (D) violent |
| _____ | 8. (A) married | (B) united | (C) tolerated | (D) sprained |
| _____ | 9. (A) negative | (B) positive | (C) optimistic | (D) pessimistic |
| _____ | 10. (A) whatever | (B) abroad | (C) worldwide | (D) locally |

完成日期：_____

*No gain without pain.*

吃得苦中苦，方為人上人。

信心指數
☆☆☆☆☆

## I. Vocabulary

_____ 1. A new skyscraper is going to be built on the _____.

    (A) site      (B) campaign      (C) development      (D) elevator

_____ 2. The car is _____ speed. It is going faster and faster.

    (A) reducing      (B) chasing      (C) preparing      (D) gathering

_____ 3. A _____ society should be tolerant and allow the existence of different ideas and beliefs.

    (A) conservative      (B) radical      (C) traditional      (D) liberal

_____ 4. I think you'll find it _____ to pay with a credit card.

    (A) adventurous      (B) advantageous      (C) exhausted      (D) relaxing

_____ 5. The wooden bridge is too weak to _____ the heavy truck.

    (A) interpret      (B) support      (C) invade      (D) mention

_____ 6. He is doing researches on _____ behavior.

    (A) humane      (B) human      (C) humanely      (D) human being

_____ 7. One of the _____ of staying with your parents is that you don't have to pay the rent.

    (A) disadvantages      (B) flaws      (C) merits      (D) characters

_____ 8. The famous scientist gave speeches to _____ all over the world.

    (A) humans      (B) creatures      (C) authors      (D) audience

_____ 9. I was caught in the heavy rain and got _____ to the skin.

    (A) humid      (B) dry      (C) destructive      (D) soaked

_____ 10. We all believe that the criminal will in time be brought to _____.

    (A) just      (B) justly      (C) justify      (D) justice

_____ 11. We were disappointed that the boss gave a _____ answer to our request for a raise in salary.

    (A) positive      (B) passive      (C) negative      (D) decisive

_____ 12. English has _____ many words from French and German.

    (A) borrowed      (B) lent      (C) discovered      (D) invented

_____ 13. He _____ at the bird with his rifle but he missed it.

    (A) shaved      (B) shook      (C) shifted      (D) shot

_____ 14. Ann is good at everything. She is the _____ of all her friends.

    (A) enemy      (B) fantasy      (C) property      (D) envy

_____ 15. She is a _____ person. Even her books are arranged in alphabetic order.

     (A) well-organized    (B) well-educated    (C) well-behaved    (D) well-informed

_____ 16. I don't think I can continue doing the job. It's too much _____ for me.

     (A) challenging    (B) excessive    (C) proper    (D) loose

_____ 17. _____ a tablet right now and go to bed.

     (A) Spit    (B) Splash    (C) Swallow    (D) Swear

_____ 18. The car crash was _____ by a big fire.

     (A) followed    (B) funded    (C) founded    (D) flushed

_____ 19. The earth is one of the _____ that move around the sun.

     (A) orbits    (B) stars    (C) globes    (D) planets

_____ 20. The tooth doesn't exactly hurt but I am _____ of it.

     (A) conscience    (B) embarrassed    (C) slight    (D) conscious

## II. Idioms & Phrases

_____ 1. The doctor scribbled the prescription on a piece of paper, and the pharmacist could barely _____ what was written.

     (A) work on    (B) make out    (C) clean out    (D) move out

_____ 2. Even if both sides agree to stop the fire, how can they _____ neither of them will break the agreement?

     (A) look for    (B) take up    (C) make certain    (D) stand for

_____ 3. She is kind and sympathetic. If I were _____, I would not give him any money.

     (A) in reality    (B) in her shoes    (C) in case    (D) in question

_____ 4. I _____ snakes. They scare me.

     (A) am drilled into          (B) am driven off

     (C) have a dread of        (D) am dressed up as

_____ 5. I will not lend him so much money. Anyway, he is just _____.

     (A) a nodding acquaintance      (B) a friend for life

     (C) my bosom friend          (D) a blood brother

_____ 6. Her mother _____ her for she came home late at night.

     (A) was capable of         (B) was bound to

     (C) was enthusiastic about    (D) was angry with

_____ 7. John and I _____ driving, so both of us could get more rests.

     (A) took turns          (B) made sense to

     (C) depended on        (D) took advantage of

_____ 8. He tried hard to _____ his anger.

(A) push back      (B) hold back      (C) hit back      (D) look back

_____ 9. As a typhoon is approaching, we _____ make some preparations in advance.

     (A) suppose to      (B) are likely to      (C) had better      (D) tend to

_____ 10. I got the job completely _____ . I happened to be the only applicant.

     (A) with difficulty      (B) by chance      (C) off hand      (D) at present

# III. Cloze Test

## Part A

The atmosphere is a layer of gases around the earth. This layer, ___1___ a blanket, makes the earth warm enough for life and provide the air we breathe. Earth is the only one of all the ___2___ we know about which has the right temperature for life. If the climate becomes too hot or too cold, life on earth cannot continue to ___3___ . But scientists have a ___4___ that a lot of carbon dioxide in the atmosphere will act like the glass in a greenhouse. As the sun shines through the carbon dioxide blanket, the atmosphere will get hotter and hotter. Scientists ___5___ that as a result of more carbon dioxide in the atmosphere, there will be a global warming, or a long-term ___6___ in temperature over the earth. The results of a global warming will cause the ice to ___7___ at the North and South ___8___ . If this happens, ocean ___9___ will rise and flood cities on the coast of continents. Everyone who lives on earth must make some decisions about the possible greenhouse effect. As the population of the world grows, we must be more careful about the effect our " ___10___ " is having on the earth.

_____ 1. (A) like      (B) liking      (C) alike      (D) likely

_____ 2. (A) objects      (B) satellites      (C) planets      (D) comets

_____ 3. (A) exit      (B) exist      (C) excite      (D) exhibit

_____ 4. (A) reason      (B) project      (C) theory      (D) vision

_____ 5. (A) protest      (B) present      (C) prevent      (D) predict

_____ 6. (A) rise      (B) raise      (C) lift      (D) promotion

_____ 7. (A) melt      (B) dissolve      (C) vanish      (D) vaporize

_____ 8. (A) Polls      (B) Poles      (C) Posts      (D) Ponies

_____ 9. (A) standard      (B) flat      (C) degree      (D) level

_____ 10. (A) process      (B) progress      (C) program      (D) procedure

## Part B

The skin which covers the tips of the fingers and thumbs is crossed by numerous ridges arranged in different patterns. These patterns are ___1___ from birth and remain exactly the same ___2___ a person's life, even when the skin becomes ___3___ and cracked as a result of

old age. Such patterns are never ___4___ from parents to children, and no one in the world has the same patterns as anyone ___5___. Even ___6___ twins have different sets of fingerprints. ___7___, fingerprints offer a most ___8___ and foolproof way of identifying people.

Any ridged part of the hand and the foot may be used as a ___9___ of identification, but finger impressions are usually ___10___ since they can be taken easily and quickly.

_____ 1. (A) permanent    (B) various    (C) temporary    (D) sticky

_____ 2. (A) for    (B) to    (C) throughout    (D) with

_____ 3. (A) smooth    (B) wrinkled    (C) slippery    (D) twinkled

_____ 4. (A) set out    (B) put off    (C) thrown away    (D) passed on

_____ 5. (A) else    (B) who    (C) others    (D) that

_____ 6. (A) identical    (B) diverse    (C) fertile    (D) graceful

_____ 7. (A) As a result    (B) However

       (C) By the way    (D) On the other hand

_____ 8. (A) useless    (B) useful    (C) used    (D) using

_____ 9. (A) motivation    (B) monster    (C) mercy    (D) means

_____ 10. (A) disgusted    (B) inferior    (C) selective    (D) preferred

完成日期：_____

實戰語錄

*Practice makes perfect.*
熟能生巧。

## I. Vocabulary

_____ 1. It is not easy for an old man to climb up such a _____ cliff.

    (A) steep     (B) steady     (C) stable     (D) standard

_____ 2. He _____ long upon the old woman's face.

    (A) glimpsed     (B) glanced     (C) gazed     (D) grabbed

_____ 3. People in a democratic country may not understand the true meaning of _____ and tend to abuse it and trespass against others.

    (A) education     (B) liberty     (C) affection     (D) loyalty

_____ 4. The football team's performance was _____ by the rain.

    (A) reduced     (B) injured     (C) admitted     (D) affected

_____ 5. A _____ Taiwan summer is hot and humid.

    (A) minor     (B) naked     (C) typical     (D) passive

_____ 6. The mechanic is able to solve every _____ problem in my car.

    (A) imagine     (B) imaginable     (C) imaginative     (D) imaginary

_____ 7. I have a habit of listening to the _____ on the answering machine as soon as I get home.

    (A) letters     (B) messages     (C) information     (D) words

_____ 8. Bob is not _____ at present. Should I ask him to call you back?

    (A) affordable     (B) victorious     (C) destructive     (D) available

_____ 9. Seeing his father come in, he _____ his topic of conversation immediately.

    (A) switched     (B) swept     (C) stitched     (D) supposed

_____ 10. He tore the _____ of his trousers.

    (A) elbows     (B) shoulders     (C) knees     (D) ankles

_____ 11. The parents were accused of _____ their children because they failed to provide them with proper food and care.

    (A) dominating     (B) tolerating     (C) spoiling     (D) neglecting

_____ 12. I started up my own business and now I am my own _____.

    (A) operator     (B) boss     (C) trainer     (D) student

_____ 13. The news came from a reliable _____. It can be highly true.

    (A) source     (B) rumor     (C) legend     (D) verse

_____ 14. His job is to _____ how a new material stands up to wear and tear.

    (A) evaluate     (B) recycle     (C) progress     (D) approve

_____ 15. The nice restaurant on the bank of the river was _____ a boathouse.

(A) originally      (B) automatically      (C) conclusively      (D) intensively

_____ 16. They held their wedding _____ at the nearby church.

(A) parade      (B) demonstration      (C) ceremony      (D) procession

_____ 17. The road was very _____. I could hardly stand still.

(A) solid      (B) slippery      (C) steep      (D) stiff

_____ 18. Politics is a(n) _____ topic in my home. We never talk about it.

(A) current      (B) main      (C) inviting      (D) forbidden

_____ 19. The train is to leave at _____ 4 at three o'clock sharp.

(A) Stage      (B) Board      (C) Platform      (D) Landing

_____ 20. The fire caused _____ damage to the building.

(A) constructive      (B) considerable      (C) considerate      (D) constant

## II. Idioms & Phrases

_____ 1. In the _____, the mother-to-be received a gift of 24-hour free baby-sitting.

(A) baby shower      (B) baby boom      (C) baby face      (D) baby goods

_____ 2. The drought _____ all the wells.

(A) wrinkled up      (B) shut out      (C) dried up      (D) died out

_____ 3. He got on a wrong bus _____, which took him farther away from his destination.

(A) by nature      (B) by chance      (C) by luck      (D) by mistake

_____ 4. Children should do something _____ what their parents do for them.

(A) in memory of      (B) in celebration of      (C) in appreciation of      (D) in honor of

_____ 5. Not knowing what to do, the little girl _____ tears.

(A) burst out      (B) burst into      (C) ran out of      (D) blew down

_____ 6. _____ more potato chips.

(A) Help yourself to            (B) Expose yourself to

(C) Devote yourself to          (D) Engage yourself to

_____ 7. You cannot always demand your way. You should learn to _____.

(A) knock others down          (B) surrender to others

(C) meet others halfway        (D) stand on your own two feet

_____ 8. Whenever I see Mrs. Collins, she is _____ one of the neighbors.

(A) chatting with      (B) in charge of      (C) checking in      (D) catching up

_____ 9. Do you believe in love _____? I don't because sometimes the first impression is not objective.

(A) at no cost      (B) at first sight      (C) at birth      (D) at high speeds

_____ 10. Our thanks are _____ the editor.

     (A) all for      (B) due to      (C) fond of      (D) indicative of

## III. Cloze Test

### Part A

We are constantly surrounded by various sounds, natural and ___1___. Some of them are pleasant to the ear like the singing of early birds. Some are ___2___ like the roars of motorcycles. The interesting thing about sounds is that there are sounds which we cannot hear but which nevertheless have ___3___ effects upon us.

Scientists discovered that, at some ___4___ with huge stones, there were patterns of ultrasound that were strongest at dawn on any day, but ___5___ to a high frequency in March and October. They also found that circles of stones, like the famous one at Stonehenge, create an ultrasonic ___6___. There is always a background of ultrasound in the countryside produced by the ___7___ of leaves and grass. Inside the rock circles, there is sometimes complete ultrasonic ___8___. It is clear that these ancient ___9___ are not placed ___10___. Those who built them must have known what they were about.

_____ 1. (A) realistic      (B) identical      (C) artificial      (D) initial

_____ 2. (A) humorous      (B) ridiculous      (C) amazing      (D) annoying

_____ 3. (A) atomic      (B) puzzling      (C) defensible      (D) worthy

_____ 4. (A) huts      (B) apartments      (C) flats      (D) sites

_____ 5. (A) rose      (B) raised      (C) aroused      (D) arose

_____ 6. (A) barber      (B) barrel      (C) barrier      (D) bay

_____ 7. (A) beep      (B) rustle      (C) click      (D) snap

_____ 8. (A) aquarium      (B) silence      (C) calculator      (D) escalator

_____ 9. (A) feathers      (B) globes      (C) lightings      (D) structures

_____ 10. (A) at random      (B) at risk      (C) at their leisure      (D) at times

### Part B

My next-door neighbor, Raymond, is well past eighty. Although he is ___1___ in years, he has not lost his ___2___ attitude toward life. He says he enjoys every minute of his life. However, you can hardly imagine how ___3___ he lived the first two years after he retired. ___4___ to many senior citizens who are not adapted to their retirement, he became very ___5___ and discouraged, not interested in anything. He easily lost his ___6___, complained about everything and felt sick almost every day. It ___7___ that his friends and children stayed

away from him. Fortunately, one day an old friend of his visited him and changed his life. He decided to put his life ___8___. Since then, he has begun to exercise ___9___ participate in leisurely activities. His lungs, muscles and ___10___ are becoming stronger every passing day. Everybody says that he looks ten years younger than he is.

_____ 1. (A) admired    (B) advanced    (C) ambitious    (D) available

_____ 2. (A) negative    (B) positive    (C) inclusive    (D) offensive

_____ 3. (A) shortsighted    (B) fairly    (C) sympathetically    (D) miserably

_____ 4. (A) Similar    (B) Next    (C) Like    (D) Sensitive

_____ 5. (A) active    (B) passive    (C) aggressive    (D) successive

_____ 6. (A) temper    (B) humid    (C) talent    (D) crisis

_____ 7. (A) pointed out    (B) occurred to    (C) turned out    (D) referred to

_____ 8. (A) in detail    (B) in style    (C) in orbit    (D) in order

_____ 9. (A) as to    (B) such as    (C) as well as    (D) in addition to

_____ 10. (A) jaws    (B) joints    (C) cheeks    (D) brows

完成日期：_____

實戰語錄

*Take the rough with the smooth.*

處坎坷，以泰然。

## I. Vocabulary

_____ 1. The _____ form of "wives" is "wife."

    (A) unique     (B) exceptional     (C) superior     (D) singular

_____ 2. Environmentalists are against electricity _____ from nuclear power.

    (A) misery     (B) maturity     (C) generation     (D) shortage

_____ 3. A bolt of _____ struck the small cabin and started a fire.

    (A) balloon     (B) chemistry     (C) lightning     (D) rainbow

_____ 4. The dog is very _____. It barks at everyone.

    (A) ambitious     (B) aggressive     (C) agreeable     (D) admirable

_____ 5. This firm has a _____ of 50 people.

    (A) stuff     (B) stiff     (C) stage     (D) staff

_____ 6. A parrot can _____ human speech.

    (A) interpret     (B) intimate     (C) imitate     (D) interact

_____ 7. The doctor is examining the blood cells under the _____.

    (A) microscope     (B) microwave     (C) microphone     (D) microfilm

_____ 8. The university has _____ Jane a $1,000 scholarship.

    (A) presented     (B) maintained     (C) awarded     (D) awoke

_____ 9. The old man cannot walk without his _____.

    (A) trick     (B) disk     (C) stick     (D) sting

_____ 10. The earthquake was the greatest _____ we had ever experienced.

    (A) victory     (B) disaster     (C) monster     (D) shame

_____ 11. The manager had to _____ with the workers so that the strike would end as soon as possible.

    (A) negotiate     (B) compete     (C) mix     (D) struggle

_____ 12. The basketball player _____ the ball against the wall.

    (A) bounced     (B) bumped     (C) braked     (D) blessed

_____ 13. Stick a 75-cent _____ on the envelope before you mail it.

    (A) answer     (B) knot     (C) stamp     (D) gum

_____ 14. At a rough _____, I will get the work done by Tuesday.

    (A) treatment     (B) awareness     (C) estimate     (D) surroundings

_____ 15. The car has a scratch on the driver's side, but _____, it is in perfect/mint condition.

      (A) however      (B) therefore      (C) moreover      (D) otherwise

_____ 16. She is the first Olympic tennis _____ in our country.

      (A) sportsmanship      (B) champion      (C) court      (D) leader

_____ 17. My nose itches and I can't help _____.

      (A) sneezing      (B) coughing      (C) whispering      (D) yawning

_____ 18. A _____ person is always willing to forgive.

      (A) forgave      (B) forgiven      (C) forgiving      (D) forgive

_____ 19. His sense of humor has won him great _____ among friends.

      (A) popularity      (B) population      (C) pollution      (D) position

_____ 20. His behavior is not _____ with his words.

      (A) consistent      (B) linked      (C) confronted      (D) contacted

## II. Idioms & Phrases

_____ 1. With such meager earnings, it's really hard for him to _____.

      (A) come into existence      (B) get away with it

      (C) pull himself together      (D) make both ends meet

_____ 2. Don't _____ the radio _____ because I don't know how to put it together.

      (A) take...apart      (B) tell...apart      (C) keep...apart      (D) fall...apart

_____ 3. Bill _____ his old desk and bought a new one.

      (A) called off      (B) threw away      (C) threw up      (D) stirred up

_____ 4. Can I be _____ to you?

      (A) of my own growing      (B) of course

      (C) of any help      (D) of high status

_____ 5. As nobody has come to claim the stolen car, the police have to keep it _____.

      (A) in seconds      (B) for the moment      (C) ever after      (D) now and then

_____ 6. He wanted to try bungee jumping, but he _____ at last.

      (A) kept his promise      (B) lost his breath

      (C) chickened out      (D) made up his mind

_____ 7. The earth _____ an orange in shape.

      (A) is covered with      (B) is famous for      (C) is similar to      (D) is named after

_____ 8. He is _____ nervous when asking Mary to the party.

      (A) fond of      (B) thirsty for      (C) kind of      (D) keen on

_____ 9. _____ obstacle lies ahead, we will not give up.

      (A) It doesn't matter what      (B) Regarding to

      (C) No matter what      (D) With regard to

_____ 10. I enjoyed walking _____ with my husband along the riverbank.

      (A) one by one      (B) arm in arm      (C) all in all      (D) little by little

## III. Cloze Test

**Part A**

Eleven-year-old Angela was stricken with a disease involving her nervous system. She was unable to walk and her movement was _____1_____ in other ways as well. The doctors did not hold out much hope of her ever recovering from this illness. They predicted she would spend the _____2_____ of her life in a wheelchair. They said that _____3_____, if any, were able to come back to _____4_____ after contracting this disease. But the girl was undaunted. She would vow to anyone who would _____5_____ that she was definitely going to be walking again someday.

In the hospital, she was taught about imaging—about seeing herself walking. If it would do nothing else, it would _____6_____ give her hope and something positive to do in the long _____7_____ hours in her bed. One day, as she was straining with all her _____8_____ to imagine her legs moving again, it seemed as though a _____9_____ happened: the bed moved, and she herself moved. In fact, at this very _____10_____, everything moved. You see, it was the San Francisco earthquake! But Angela was convinced that she did it.

_____ 1. (A) distributed    (B) corrected    (C) instructed    (D) restricted

_____ 2. (A) remain    (B) last    (C) left    (D) rest

_____ 3. (A) few    (B) a few    (C) little    (D) a little

_____ 4. (A) common    (B) regular    (C) ordinary    (D) normal

_____ 5. (A) hear    (B) listen    (C) sound    (D) note

_____ 6. (A) at last    (B) at least    (C) at best    (D) at most

_____ 7. (A) waking    (B) awake    (C) waken    (D) wake

_____ 8. (A) might    (B) may    (C) must    (D) need

_____ 9. (A) mystery    (B) misery    (C) miracle    (D) marvel

_____ 10. (A) condition    (B) movement    (C) moment    (D) situation

**Part B**

Janice Heart is a rising star in the world of classical music. When she was a small child, a composer that she met at the Toronto Philharmonic _____1_____ her. He provided her _____2_____ the incentive, motivation, to learn how to play the piano. _____3_____ thirteen she had already memorized the works of _____4_____ such as Beethoven and Bach. She _____5_____ that she thrives at playing the piano and _____6_____ she must have annoyed her parents a lot as a child with her _____7_____ practicing. Her parents, _____8_____, were very sympathetic to Janice's dream and she

could always ___9___ them for emotional support. Janice has now mastered her ___10___ and her extraordinary music has become a sensation throughout the world.

_____ 1. (A) invited      (B) inspired      (C) inspected      (D) infected

_____ 2. (A) with      (B) into      (C) by      (D) for

_____ 3. (A) In the year of      (B) Over a period of

           (C) At the age of      (D) At the moment of

_____ 4. (A) literature      (B) limitations      (C) leisure      (D) legends

_____ 5. (A) commits      (B) permits      (C) insists      (D) admits

_____ 6. (A) how      (B) that      (C) what      (D) which

_____ 7. (A) competitive      (B) constant      (C) consistent      (D) constructive

_____ 8. (A) however      (B) for instance      (C) moreover      (D) consequently

_____ 9. (A) consist in      (B) count on      (C) conflict with      (D) comment on

_____ 10. (A) interaction      (B) instruction      (C) instrument      (D) investment

完成日期：_____

## 奮戰語錄

*Every little helps.*

積少成多。

## I. Vocabulary

_____ 1. According to the _____ of the accident, that speeding car crashed into the train.

    (A) witness     (B) volunteer     (C) scientist     (D) manufacturer

_____ 2. We can help to limit _____ warming by using cars less often.

    (A) electric     (B) global     (C) heated     (D) powerful

_____ 3. You can use water or milk for the _____ required in this recipe.

    (A) quantity     (B) liquid     (C) solid     (D) foundation

_____ 4. He is having an _____ with a married woman.

    (A) affair     (B) education     (C) union     (D) imagination

_____ 5. This part of the lake is quite _____ . The boat may touch its bottom.

    (A) peaceful     (B) explosive     (C) negative     (D) shallow

_____ 6. Your _____ of how to use computers will shut you out of the constantly changing world.

    (A) illustration     (B) innocence     (C) ignorance     (D) improvement

_____ 7. Many congressmen voted against an increase in the _____ budget because they don't believe there is any threat of war in the near future.

    (A) educational     (B) agricultural     (C) developmental     (D) military

_____ 8. I hate being the first to arrive at the party—it makes me feel _____ .

    (A) awkward     (B) pleased     (C) distracted     (D) satisfied

_____ 9. Seeing a _____ seat near the door, she came to sit there swiftly.

    (A) fertile     (B) vacant     (C) influential     (D) hasty

_____ 10. The students who misbehaved have been placed under strict _____ .

    (A) discipline     (B) influence     (C) retreat     (D) weapon

_____ 11. She lives in an unsafe _____ . There is stealing and drug-trafficking going on in the streets.

    (A) neighborhood     (B) territory     (C) landscape     (D) geography

_____ 12. You won't get any credit for giving him a hand, so why _____ ?

    (A) buy     (B) bother     (C) scare     (D) need

_____ 13. Basically, children are the real _____ of their parents' divorce.

    (A) volunteers     (B) critics     (C) victims     (D) applicants

_____ 14. With the _____ that the plane was delayed for an hour, it was a perfect trip.

    (A) inspection     (B) exception     (C) expectation     (D) reception

_____ 15. The _____ of the election won't be certain until the last votes have been counted.

(A) outline      (B) outlook      (C) outfit      (D) outcome

_____ 16. They _____ you $20 to get into the pub. You still have to pay for your drinks.

(A) change      (B) cause      (C) request      (D) charge

_____ 17. The drivers who _____ traffic rules should be punished for their misbehavior.

(A) violate      (B) follow      (C) obey      (D) license

_____ 18. I turned to Mary when I felt troubled for I regarded her as a _____ of calm.

(A) fun      (B) fountain      (C) fortune      (D) formation

_____ 19. There is still a certain percentage of the world _____ suffering from the lack of proper nutrition.

(A) people      (B) humans      (C) population      (D) pollution

_____ 20. The new telephone rates will affect all _____ and companies.

(A) consultants      (B) economists      (C) lecturers      (D) consumers

## II. Idioms & Phrases

_____ 1. The noise downstairs _____ John _____ from his nap.

(A) fed up...with      (B) regarded...as      (C) called...down      (D) woke...up

_____ 2. Bill is not _____ in any of the social sciences.

(A) in the house      (B) at home      (C) on earth      (D) in the world

_____ 3. I don't think you can lose weight if you exercise _____.

(A) on occasions      (B) once in a blue moon

(C) to date      (D) once upon a time

_____ 4. When I saw the poor little puppy, I _____ to take it home.

(A) couldn't help      (B) couldn't but      (C) couldn't help but      (D) had no choice but

_____ 5. We started to have dinner after all the guests _____.

(A) were seating      (B) sat themselves      (C) be seated      (D) seated themselves

_____ 6. The industrious people always work _____.

(A) in earnest      (B) in vain      (C) in itself      (D) in a rage

_____ 7. He is too weak to stand up, _____ run.

(A) let alone      (B) not to mention      (C) needless to say      (D) without saying

_____ 8. The robber was stopped outside of the bank and put _____.

(A) to bed      (B) under arrest      (C) in his shoes      (D) an end

_____ 9. People from _____ enjoy the great musical performance. It is very popular with everyone.

(A) odds and ends   (B) a bed of roses  (C) all walks of life  (D) the church service

_____ 10. He _____ the idea of traveling around the world. He wishes to make it come true.

    (A) gets hooked on  (B) gets adapted to (C) gets started with  (D) gets adjusted to

## III. Cloze Test

( Part A )

   Social etiquettes vary from culture to culture. As business becomes more ____1____, it is increasingly important to learn about proper behavior so that no ____2____ will be caused.

   In France, for example, it is not good ____3____ to raise tricky questions of business over the main course. Business has its ____4____: after the cheese course. Unless you are prepared to eat in silence, you have to talk about something—something, that is, ____5____ than the business deal which you are chewing over in your head.

   Italians give similar importance to the whole business entertaining. As a ____6____ of fact, as course after course appears, you entirely ____7____ the purpose of your being there. If you have the energy, you can always do the polite thing when the ____8____ finally ends, and offer to pay. Then, after a(n) ____9____ discussion, you must remember the next polite thing to do— let your host ____10____ the bill.

_____ 1. (A) universal     (B) national     (C) local     (D) international

_____ 2. (A) suspense     (B) defense     (C) offence     (D) expense

_____ 3. (A) politeness     (B) manners     (C) means     (D) ways

_____ 4. (A) part     (B) place     (C) direction     (D) location

_____ 5. (A) other     (B) more     (C) less     (D) further

_____ 6. (A) manner     (B) practice     (C) matter     (D) reality

_____ 7. (A) lose track of     (B) catch up of     (C) take charge of     (D) make up for

_____ 8. (A) business     (B) course     (C) night     (D) meal

_____ 9. (A) live     (B) living     (C) alive     (D) lively

_____ 10. (A) pick up     (B) put down     (C) pull over     (D) push away

( Part B )

   We're hearing this ____1____ "genetic engineering" with ____2____ frequency these days. For those readers who may not be sure of its meaning, some ____3____ follow. When we ____4____ genes, we are referring to chemical substances in the ____5____ of all living things that establish an organism's ____6____. Genetic engineering is the changing of certain genes, usually to ____7____ an organism in some way. In recent years, for example, certain genes have

been placed in tomato plants to make tomatoes ____8____ better and keep them fresh in supermarkets for a longer time. Cows have been ____9____ with a growth hormone that makes dairy cattle give more milk and reduces the amount of fat in the ____10____ of beef cattle.

| | | | | |
|---|---|---|---|---|
| _____ 1. | (A) engine | (B) term | (C) organ | (D) poverty |
| _____ 2. | (A) high | (B) increasing | (C) low | (D) decreasing |
| _____ 3. | (A) cautions | (B) expressions | (C) gestures | (D) definitions |
| _____ 4. | (A) speak of | (B) run down | (C) pick on | (D) hang up |
| _____ 5. | (A) brains | (B) blood | (C) cells | (D) stomachs |
| _____ 6. | (A) references | (B) characteristics | (C) entries | (D) gangsters |
| _____ 7. | (A) improve | (B) forgive | (C) insert | (D) joint |
| _____ 8. | (A) sound | (B) launch | (C) maintain | (D) taste |
| _____ 9. | (A) knocked | (B) nested | (C) offended | (D) treated |
| _____ 10. | (A) knee | (B) meat | (C) oil | (D) bone |

完成日期：＿＿＿＿＿＿＿＿

實戰語錄

*Every man is his own worst enemy.*

欲勝人者先自勝。

信心指數
☆☆☆☆☆

# I. Vocabulary

_____ 1. How many points does a touchdown _____?

(A) scout      (B) scold      (C) score      (D) scrub

_____ 2. He _____ in his success.

(A) gloried      (B) glory      (C) glorious      (D) gloriously

_____ 3. In many states of America, it is illegal to sell _____ to people under 21.

(A) automobiles      (B) grocery      (C) animals      (D) liquor

_____ 4. Three enemy _____ have been shot down over the borderline.

(A) vessels      (B) vehicles      (C) aircraft      (D) trains

_____ 5. The baby's skin is as _____ as silk.

(A) tough      (B) stiff      (C) smooth      (D) straight

_____ 6. More and more people plan to _____ into a country where there are far fewer political disputes.

(A) migrate      (B) immigrate      (C) emigrate      (D) emerge

_____ 7. She dreamed of marrying a _____ and enjoying a life of ease and luxury ever after.

(A) candidate      (B) millionaire      (C) journalist      (D) technician

_____ 8. I take as little _____ as possible with me when I travel.

(A) chocolate      (B) nylon      (C) baggage      (D) wreck

_____ 9. She _____ with relief when the work was done.

(A) sighed      (B) imagined      (C) noted      (D) hesitated

_____ 10. She made no _____ of her feelings. She did not hide her feelings.

(A) fun      (B) mistake      (C) exploration      (D) disguise

_____ 11. The baseball game is broadcast in every part of the country through a national television _____.

(A) network      (B) framework      (C) artwork      (D) glasswork

_____ 12. She is used to wearing this _____ of perfume.

(A) brass      (B) brain      (C) breast      (D) brand

_____ 13. We should learn to look on the bright _____ of life. Be optimistic all the time.

(A) slice      (B) piece      (C) sheet      (D) side

_____ 14. Our supply of food is _____. We have nothing to eat now.

(A) discouraged      (B) exhausted      (C) frozen      (D) preserved

15. In dealing with his assignment, he tends to be too optimistic and _____ the possible difficulties ahead.

    (A) overtake       (B) overthrow       (C) overpass       (D) overlook

16. He donated most of his income to a local _____ to help the poor.

    (A) newspaper       (B) barn       (C) charity       (D) mansion

17. A _____ is a large sports ground with seats all around.

    (A) studio       (B) strip       (C) statue       (D) stadium

18. I am _____. May I borrow your coat?

    (A) freeze       (B) freezing       (C) freezer       (D) frozen

19. When he travels on business, he always brings a _____ computer with him.

    (A) movable       (B) portable       (C) mobile       (D) replaceable

20. If you don't know the meaning of the word, you can guess what it is by reading the _____.

    (A) concert       (B) context       (C) comments       (D) contract

## II. Idioms & Phrases

1. Who can _____ Mike's girlfriend to let her realize how disgusting Mike is?

    (A) invent a new story for       (B) break the news to

    (C) hide the truth from       (D) tell a lie to

2. _____ will her father agree with her marrying the stranger.

    (A) Under no circumstances       (B) In this condition

    (C) By all means       (D) On any account

3. I _____ the people who hurt me. They had to pay for that.

    (A) took part in     (B) took shelter from     (C) took revenge on     (D) took care of

4. The doctor made the excited feel _____.

    (A) at work       (B) at present       (C) at ease       (D) at best

5. We walked all the way to the train station _____ took a taxi.

    (A) instead of       (B) without even       (C) other than       (D) rather than

6. _____ news, I hardly watch any television.

    (A) In addition to     (B) Regardless of     (C) Except for     (D) In spite of

7. She _____ me, saying "Goodbye."

    (A) served as       (B) waved at       (C) got along with       (D) counted on

8. We held the dinner _____ a fellow teacher who was going to retire.

    (A) in memory of     (B) in celebration of     (C) in honor of     (D) in the hope of

9. The wife is complaining that her husband is _____.

(A) ill at ease (B) good at everything

(C) doing good (D) good for nothing

_____ 10. I hope the weather will have _____ by this afternoon because we have a football game.

(A) cleaned up (B) cleared off (C) cleared up (D) cleaned out

## III. Cloze Test

**Part A**

The philosophy of The Body Shop is different from that of most cosmetics companies. It does not ____1____ miracles or ever-lasting youth. The Body Shop develops its line of high ____2____ and sensible products by using traditional wisdom, herbal ____3____, and modern technology.

The Body Shop does not believe in ____4____ without principles. The respect for the ____5____ is one of the Body Shop's most basic principles. The company uses as little packaging ____6____ to conserve natural resources and ____7____ waste. Customers are encouraged to bring their old ____8____ to refill them. If they do this, they get a discount on their next ____9____. The Body Shop is also strongly ____10____ to animal testing in the cosmetics industry. It never tests its products or ingredients on animals.

_____ 1. (A) promise (B) invent (C) preserve (D) interfere

_____ 2. (A) probability (B) quality (C) label (D) mark

_____ 3. (A) review (B) physician (C) favor (D) knowledge

_____ 4. (A) profits (B) exports (C) imports (D) intuition

_____ 5. (A) customs (B) environment (C) tradition (D) experiment

_____ 6. (A) as well (B) as necessary (C) as possible (D) as usual

_____ 7. (A) promote (B) discourage (C) shorten (D) reduce

_____ 8. (A) outfits (B) cosmetics (C) containers (D) clothing

_____ 9. (A) purchase (B) champion (C) shower (D) proposal

_____ 10. (A) subjected (B) adapted (C) objected (D) opposed

**Part B**

Many students would agree that listening is a difficult ____1____. For most, it is much harder to ____2____ new material by listening to a lecturer than by reading a(n) ____3____. Since listening, like reading, is a popular ____4____ of learning both in and out of school, it is important to understand why listening well is so difficult.

When listening, the students have to learn the ____5____ between the spoken and written

forms of the language. Students often ____6____ to understand the spoken form of an utterance which they recognize perfectly well in its written form. Besides, the students have to ____7____ to the speed of the speakers. If they speak very ____8____, the students may not be able to take in all that they say. ____9____, if they are very slow and deliberate, students may find it hard to keep their mind on what the speakers are saying, because their mind's ____10____ is much more rapid than that of any speaker.

| | | | | | | |
|---|---|---|---|---|---|---|
| _____ | 1. (A) talent | (B) gift | (C) genius | (D) skill |
| _____ | 2. (A) master | (B) produce | (C) govern | (D) lay |
| _____ | 3. (A) bulletin | (B) textbook | (C) advertisement | (D) announcement |
| _____ | 4. (A) network | (B) occupation | (C) method | (D) panel |
| _____ | 5. (A) conflict | (B) similarity | (C) imitation | (D) relationship |
| _____ | 6. (A) fail | (B) object | (C) enable | (D) promise |
| _____ | 7. (A) adjust | (B) admit | (C) apply | (D) refresh |
| _____ | 8. (A) softly | (B) loudly | (C) tenderly | (D) rapidly |
| _____ | 9. (A) For one thing | | (B) For another | |
| | (C) On the one hand | | (D) On the other hand | |
| _____ | 10. (A) range | (B) depth | (C) pace | (D) content |

完成日期：_____

挑戰語錄

*Never put off till tomorrow what may be done today.*

今日事，今日畢。

信心指數
☆☆☆☆☆

# I. Vocabulary

_____ 1. We went to the _____ in the National Concert Hall. It was great.

    (A) sympathy     (B) symphony     (C) harmony     (D) routine

_____ 2. She is very fond of _____ about the neighbors.

    (A) communicating     (B) quarreling     (C) gossiping     (D) fighting

_____ 3. Her latest collection of poems has received favorable reviews from _____ critics.

    (A) literary     (B) library     (C) laboratory     (D) loyalty

_____ 4. She screamed as loudly as she could to give the _____ about the fire.

    (A) force     (B) litter     (C) motion     (D) alarm

_____ 5. She is not young; I see her face _____ with age.

    (A) wrinkled     (B) exposed     (C) estimated     (D) wondered

_____ 6. The _____ of science on society is great.

    (A) affect     (B) pat     (C) attack     (D) impact

_____ 7. All the workers in this country are guaranteed a _____ wage, and they must not be paid less than that.

    (A) maximum     (B) minimum     (C) most     (D) least

_____ 8. She can make bread and cakes because she used to work in a local _____.

    (A) factory     (B) station     (C) market     (D) bakery

_____ 9. I bought some postcards and little statues as _____ of my trip to Rome.

    (A) souvenirs     (B) strategies     (C) subjects     (D) solutions

_____ 10. Israel came into _____ after World War II.

    (A) use     (B) destruction     (C) charge     (D) existence

_____ 11. John is very skillful at fixing things around the house, and therefore, is _____ "Mr. Handy."

    (A) recognized     (B) labeled     (C) characterized     (D) nicknamed

_____ 12. I had to rest for a few minutes to catch my _____ back.

    (A) sight     (B) breathe     (C) bracelet     (D) breath

_____ 13. Most students in Taiwan are supposed to go to school in _____.

    (A) umbrellas     (B) uniforms     (C) universities     (D) union

_____ 14. Those who failed to _____ their job obligations were dismissed from their jobs.

    (A) fill     (B) deal     (C) fulfill     (D) drill

_____ 15. This prize will be awarded to any _____ works in the scientific world.

(A) abandoned      (B) evident      (C) unfortunate      (D) outstanding

_____ 16. The police car was going so fast. It must have been _____ somebody.

     (A) searching      (B) chasing      (C) comforting      (D) stressing

_____ 17. The knife is very _____. It may cut your fingers.

     (A) sharp      (B) smooth      (C) rusty      (D) evident

_____ 18. She _____ the idea as not worth thinking about.

     (A) admitted      (B) dismissed      (C) missed      (D) committed

_____ 19. You must pay for the _____ when you send a letter.

     (A) poster      (B) postscript      (C) postage      (D) postman

_____ 20. The invention of Cat's eye made a major _____ to road safety.

     (A) decision      (B) distribution      (C) contribution      (D) effort

## II. Idioms & Phrases

_____ 1. Have you heard the _____ "Twinkle, twinkle, little stars" before?

     (A) chanting spell                 (B) nursery rhyme

     (C) side dish                     (D) foundation stone

_____ 2. My father is _____ his time and money. He never wastes them.

     (A) equal to      (B) grateful for      (C) economical of      (D) independent of

_____ 3. It _____ me that we could get Father a new razor for his birthday present.

     (A) flashed into      (B) hit upon      (C) struck to      (D) occurred to

_____ 4. I'd rather not _____ myself _____ too many political activities.

     (A) accuse...of      (B) associate...with      (C) combine...with      (D) release...from

_____ 5. I am _____. I need to see a doctor.

     (A) under the weather    (B) in shape      (C) on duty      (D) on the job

_____ 6. The police have been _____ the missing child in the woods for two days.

     (A) hunting for      (B) appealing to      (C) chasing with      (D) running around

_____ 7. Being defeated in the game, my brother was _____.

     (A) in action      (B) with care      (C) in a pet      (D) ins and outs

_____ 8. This is an electronic watch. You don't have to _____ and it will keep running.

     (A) call it off      (B) wind it up      (C) give it away      (D) watch it over

_____ 9. It took me an hour to _____ the annoying salesman.

     (A) let go of      (B) get rid of      (C) get the better of    (D) get close to

_____ 10. The medicine _____ my heart, which is now beating very fast.

     (A) has a strong effect on            (B) cures me of

     (C) gets rid of                     (D) puts an end to

## III. Cloze Test

### Part A

The modern Olympic Games are different from the early Olympics ___1___ two important ways. ___2___, the ancient Olympic Games used to be held to honor Zeus but modern Olympic Games no longer have any connection with ___3___. Second, the Games are no longer ___4___ to Greeks. They are international. The number of athletes taking part is over ten thousand and the number of people who will ___5___ is predicted to reach 3.5 billion. However, the main ___6___ of the Olympic Games remains the same. The Games are intended to ___7___ world peace, mutual understanding and cooperation between nations and ___8___ of the world. Every four years, athletes ___9___ in games except for three times during times of war. Sometimes particular countries have chosen not to send their athletes to Olympics. In this way, they make a ___10___ statement of some sort to the world.

_____ 1. (A) in      (B) on      (C) at      (D) by

_____ 2. (A) First of all        (B) Generally speaking

     (C) Most important of all     (D) In short

_____ 3. (A) sports    (B) honor    (C) tradition    (D) religion

_____ 4. (A) narrowed   (B) limited    (C) attached    (D) prohibited

_____ 5. (A) switch off   (B) tune in    (C) turn on    (D) hand down

_____ 6. (A) objection   (B) destination   (C) target    (D) goal

_____ 7. (A) promote    (B) protest    (C) provide    (D) propose

_____ 8. (A) trades    (B) faiths    (C) schools    (D) nations

_____ 9. (A) fight     (B) race     (C) compete    (D) match

_____ 10. (A) political   (B) economical   (C) educational   (D) financial

### Part B

In the old days, many people ___1___ plagues because infectious diseases were ___2___ through the water supply. Even today, people are at risk of drinking polluted water. We all know that water pollution can affect the ___3___ of our drinking water to such a degree that water becomes unsafe to drink. Even water that looks clean can be polluted. It may be ___4___ with germs and dangerous chemicals that we can't see. However, most people do not stop to think about the ___5___ polluted water can have on our health.

Groundwater is water that fills the ___6___ and pore spaces in rocks and sediments under the Earth's ___7___. It is a particularly valuable resource, for it ___8___ approximately ninety percent of the world's ___9___ supply or drinkable water. In Taiwan 24 percent of our drinking water comes from groundwater sources. In view of this, how can we ___10___ groundwater pollution?

| | | | |
|---|---|---|---|
| _____ 1. (A) died out | (B) died away | (C) died of | (D) died for |
| _____ 2. (A) transmitted | (B) transferred | (C) transported | (D) translated |
| _____ 3. (A) quantity | (B) quality | (C) qualification | (D) quarter |
| _____ 4. (A) loaded | (B) equipped | (C) coupled | (D) exchanged |
| _____ 5. (A) affect | (B) stress | (C) impact | (D) pressure |
| _____ 6. (A) canes | (B) crayons | (C) camels | (D) cracks |
| _____ 7. (A) surface | (B) dirt | (C) horizon | (D) volcano |
| _____ 8. (A) holds up | (B) slows down | (C) speeds up | (D) takes up |
| _____ 9. (A) partial | (B) majority | (C) total | (D) overnight |
| _____ 10. (A) catch up | (B) get rid of | (C) keep track of | (D) lose sight of |

完成日期：_____

*As you sow, so shall you reap.*

種瓜得瓜，種豆得豆。

## I. Vocabulary

_____ 1. The famous _____ has performed several successful operations.

    (A) surgeon      (B) agent      (C) customer      (D) architect

_____ 2. She danced so _____ that we all fixed our eyes on her.

    (A) gradually      (B) gracefully      (C) intensively      (D) closely

_____ 3. The salvage team used sonar to _____ the sunken ship.

    (A) locate      (B) present      (C) target      (D) gather

_____ 4. Most wines contain 10% to 15% _____.

    (A) liquid      (B) alcohol      (C) seeds      (D) water

_____ 5. His hot temper doesn't _____ him to teaching.

    (A) examine      (B) distinguish      (C) suit      (D) confuse

_____ 6. I was much _____ with his interesting story.

    (A) enjoyed      (B) marked      (C) impressed      (D) discouraged

_____ 7. The interests and benefits of the _____ groups should be respected and protected.

    (A) minority      (B) privileged      (C) superior      (D) distinguished

_____ 8. As he was getting _____, he looked much older than his real age.

    (A) crazy      (B) bald      (C) hasty      (D) bold

_____ 9. Look _____ ahead and you can see the post office on your left.

    (A) strict      (B) strange      (C) straight      (D) strong

_____ 10. The courageous boy _____ no fear.

    (A) played      (B) displayed      (C) delayed      (D) lay

_____ 11. The girl woke up from a terrifying _____ and couldn't stop crying.

    (A) fantasy      (B) accident      (C) daydream      (D) nightmare

_____ 12. He pressed his foot down hard on the _____, but to his horror the car did not slow down.

    (A) brake      (B) plate      (C) trunk      (D) break

_____ 13. The earth is one of the planets of the solar _____.

    (A) surroundings      (B) circumstance      (C) system      (D) appointment

_____ 14. To the _____ that you can arouse in your students a will to study further, you are a success as teacher.

    (A) extent      (B) extension      (C) extreme      (D) expert

_____ 15. Don't forget to pay back the money you _____ me.

(A) borrow       (B) lend       (C) loan       (D) owe

_____ 16. I will always _____ the memories of the years I spent with you at school.

(A) remind       (B) cherish       (C) memorize       (D) recite

_____ 17. Why did the police _____ him? I know he is innocent.

(A) confirm       (B) support       (C) suspect       (D) approve

_____ 18. _____ with a torch and a raincoat, they went for a walk at night.

(A) Furnished       (B) Flushed       (C) Hushed       (D) Polished

_____ 19. We decide to _____ the meeting until the manager is back from his vacation.

(A) postpone       (B) delay       (C) delete       (D) revolve

_____ 20. He tried to _____ in his speech how honored he felt to be invited.

(A) tell       (B) transfer       (C) convey       (D) gather

## II. Idioms & Phrases

_____ 1. When the shoes are _____, you can get them at a lower price.

(A) for sale       (B) on sale       (C) on the market       (D) in the market

_____ 2. If you don't _____ now, you won't be able to follow him.

(A) lose your way       (B) pay attention       (C) catch his eye       (D) lose sight

_____ 3. _____ your help, I can see through the difficulty.

(A) Thanks to       (B) In spite of       (C) But for       (D) Regardless of

_____ 4. Do you _____ the main character's struggle?

(A) illustrate with       (B) jam with       (C) identify with       (D) manage with

_____ 5. I am not the person in charge, so I am _____ to give orders.

(A) irresponsible for       (B) on purpose       (C) in no possession       (D) in no position

_____ 6. We should not take the road because it was _____ by a landslide.

(A) blocked up       (B) set up       (C) looked up       (D) showed up

_____ 7. Can you come to my office _____? I have an urgent thing to tell you.

(A) in season       (B) right away       (C) without doubt       (D) with ease

_____ 8. It is his wife who is _____ running the store. He is busy with other business.

(A) in exchange for       (B) in low spirits       (C) in high esteem       (D) in effect

_____ 9. After many years, the famous painting is now _____ a private collector.

(A) come into the possession of       (B) taken possession of

(C) in the possession of       (D) in possession of

_____ 10. My income is rather variable, but I earn $50,000 a year _____.

(A) on average       (B) above average

(C) below average            (D) about the average

## III. Cloze Test

**Part A**

Most people feel lonely sometimes. ____1____ agree that one important factor in loneliness is a person's social contacts. We ____2____ on various people for different reasons. ____3____, our families give us ____4____ support, our parents and teachers give us guidance, and our friends ____5____ similar interests and activities. However, it has been found that the ____6____ of social contacts we have is not the only reason for loneliness. It is more important how many social contacts we ____7____ we should have. ____8____, though lonely people may have many social contacts, they sometimes feel they should have ____9____. They ____10____ their own popularity.

_____ 1. (A) Philosophers    (B) Photographers    (C) Physicists    (D) Psychologists

_____ 2. (A) depend    (B) defend    (C) demand    (D) descend

_____ 3. (A) For one thing    (B) For instance    (C) For good    (D) For long

_____ 4. (A) physical    (B) mental    (C) emotional    (D) spiritual

_____ 5. (A) divide    (B) give    (C) obtain    (D) share

_____ 6. (A) number    (B) quantity    (C) amount    (D) sum

_____ 7. (A) expect    (B) enjoy    (C) thirst    (D) want

_____ 8. (A) In other way            (B) In other words

         (C) On top of that          (D) On the other hand

_____ 9. (A) all    (B) less    (C) more    (D) none

_____ 10. (A) ask    (B) inquire    (C) wonder    (D) question

**Part B**

In the past, performers, politicians, and other people in the ____1____ eye were the only people who worried about the right to a private life. Now, however, even ____2____ people are complaining about losing their privacy. They say that they have the right to be ____3____ and that now, because of technology, it is getting too easy to ____4____ this right.

People are ____5____ that companies and other organizations know so much about them. Computers have ____6____ on military service, health, school grades, and work performance. People are beginning to ask why these organizations need all this information. They are also concerned because ____7____ can now get this information without telling them. It is not ____8____, then, that more and more people are worried about invasion of privacy. As a result, they are asking all organizations to respect the ____9____ between the public's right to know and

the ___10___ right to privacy.

_____ 1. (A) private   (B) secret   (C) curious   (D) public

_____ 2. (A) intelligent   (B) considerate   (C) ordinary   (D) dominant

_____ 3. (A) poured in   (B) left alone   (C) taken part in   (D) made up for

_____ 4. (A) violate   (B) peep   (C) pardon   (D) mend

_____ 5. (A) angry   (B) welcome   (C) fond   (D) uncertain

_____ 6. (A) websites   (B) homepages   (C) documents   (D) records

_____ 7. (A) investigators   (B) examinees   (C) composers   (D) participants

_____ 8. (A) moral   (B) nightmare   (C) surprising   (D) plentiful

_____ 9. (A) merit   (B) balance   (C) mustache   (D) pilgrim

_____ 10. (A) group's   (B) union's   (C) team's   (D) individual's

完成日期：_____

*There is no royal road to learning.*
學海無涯，惟勤是岸。

## I. Vocabulary

_____ 1. Out of _____, out of mind. When you don't see the thing, you will forget all about it.

(A) fight      (B) knight      (C) might      (D) sight

_____ 2. A clever businessman will _____ at any chance to make a profit.

(A) struggle      (B) look      (C) grasp      (D) thirst

_____ 3. In persuasive writing, you have to provide enough _____ argument to support your points of view.

(A) literary      (B) logical      (C) fashionable      (D) pleasant

_____ 4. People here are very _____ to the dangers of operating a nuclear power plant.

(A) alert      (B) aware      (C) conscious      (D) frightened

_____ 5. Strong coffee enables me to _____ awake.

(A) consider      (B) apply      (C) stay      (D) quit

_____ 6. Your test scores _____ that you had worked very hard.

(A) supplied      (B) implied      (C) applied      (D) replied

_____ 7. You should not expect any _____. Success will come only through hard work.

(A) marvels      (B) miracles      (C) mysteries      (D) mistakes

_____ 8. The kid fell and his mother offered to put a _____ on his knee.

(A) bandage      (B) cover      (C) cast      (D) cone

_____ 9. She _____ perfume everywhere to cover the bad smell.

(A) dyed      (B) observed      (C) dismissed      (D) sprayed

_____ 10. The question was hotly _____ in the meeting.

(A) burned      (B) worried      (C) exercised      (D) disputed

_____ 11. His theory about the end of the world is complete _____ to me. I don't believe a word of it.

(A) logic      (B) evidence      (C) experience      (D) nonsense

_____ 12. He was so _____ as to risk his life to rescue the children.

(A) shameless      (B) timid      (C) brave      (D) concerned

_____ 13. The _____ erupted violently yesterday. The nearby villages were covered with ash.

(A) waterfall      (B) circumstance      (C) landslide      (D) volcano

_____ 14. My parents were both musicians. I was _____ to music very early.

(A) recorded      (B) touched      (C) contacted      (D) exposed

_____ 15. I have only made some general comments. Don't take them _____.

(A) privately      (B) personally      (C) directly      (D) individually

_____ 16. The birds, _____ noisily, woke us up at daybreak.

(A) banging      (B) murmuring      (C) whistling      (D) chirping

_____ 17. They _____ at the unexpected guest in great amazement.

(A) reduced      (B) managed      (C) stared      (D) abandoned

_____ 18. After her children grew up, she went to a college for _____ education.

(A) simple      (B) private      (C) further      (D) public

_____ 19. With the rapid development of modern technology, it is really hard to _____ what life will be like after 50 years.

(A) predict      (B) present      (C) pretend      (D) prefer

_____ 20. It's useless trying to _____ her that she doesn't need to lose weight.

(A) convince      (B) converse      (C) contrast      (D) encourage

## II. Idioms & Phrases

_____ 1. The living room also _____ our dining place.

(A) is named after      (B) speaks of      (C) serves as      (D) thinks of

_____ 2. _____ you are walking on the moon.

(A) Only if      (B) Provided that      (C) What a relief      (D) Imagine that

_____ 3. The weather was nice and sunny, but _____, dark clouds collected and it started to rain.

(A) all in all      (B) all at once      (C) out of the blue      (D) all over

_____ 4. During the summer vacation, we traveled across America _____.

(A) from door to door      (B) from generation to generation

(C) from coast to coast      (D) from person to person

_____ 5. It is quite late now. Could you _____ to the station?

(A) give me a ride      (B) get me a ride      (C) give me up      (D) go in for me

_____ 6. There is _____ truth in his story. Part of what he said is true.

(A) an element of      (B) a slice of      (C) a ray of      (D) a flash of

_____ 7. What time will the meeting _____?

(A) be in place      (B) be in the place      (C) take the place      (D) take place

_____ 8. My mom is back. You'd better leave _____.

(A) with amazement      (B) sooner or later

(C) in this way      (D) as soon as possible

_____ 9. He is a person who expresses ideas _____ action.

    (A) in contrast with   (B) in question of   (C) in terms of   (D) in sight of

_____ 10. I was _____ that he agreed with us.

    (A) under the control             (B) under the name

    (C) under the influence          (D) under the impression

## III. Cloze Test

### Part A

There are different ideas about pets in different parts of the world. In most cultures, animals have a(n) ___1___ position to human beings. In some instances, however, people treat their pets like ___2___ of their families, or perhaps better. In the United States, there is a very rich cat who ___3___ one hundred thousand dollars when his owner died. ___4___, the owner ___5___ the cat a very beautiful mansion to live in.

Of course, in most parts of the world, pets don't live in such wealth and ___6___. There is a more ___7___ and functional attitude toward pets. People own cats and dogs because they keep away ___8___ and other unwanted animals. Certainly, owners generally have some ___9___ feelings for their pets. However, they do not see them as ___10___ to family members.

_____ 1. (A) superior     (B) inferior     (C) junior     (D) senior

_____ 2. (A) members     (B) numbers     (C) people     (D) partners

_____ 3. (A) inhabited     (B) intimidated     (C) insured     (D) inherited

_____ 4. (A) Therefore     (B) Nonetheless     (C) Otherwise     (D) Moreover

_____ 5. (A) kept     (B) stayed     (C) left     (D) remained

_____ 6. (A) misery     (B) luxury     (C) mercy     (D) charity

_____ 7. (A) material     (B) practical     (C) economical     (D) truthful

_____ 8. (A) cattle     (B) sheep     (C) deer     (D) mice

_____ 9. (A) affectionate     (B) passionate     (C) compassionate     (D) obstinate

_____ 10. (A) the same     (B) equal     (C) match     (D) fair

### Part B

Be thin! Be ___1___! Be perfect! Get style! We are bombarded with hundreds of images a day telling us what we're supposed to look like ___2___ be okay. No one walks through normal life looking airbrushed all the time, but somehow the ___3___ makes us think we should—that if we don't, there's something wrong with us. We are so overfocused on how we look that we're terrified to look in the ___4___ and be who we are. That's why so many of us have distorted body images—that is, we look perfectly okay but we feel ___5___ we don't.

Some of us ____6____ put our health at risk by ____7____ ourselves to chase the ____8____ of looking perfect than to be who we are. This is so ____9____ —it can lead us to the disease of eating disorders. Beauty is ultimately an inside job. We need to give ourselves a break from this crazy mania about looking perfect and ____10____ some better values.

_____ 1. (A) fit    (B) fat    (C) fad    (D) fake

_____ 2. (A) on all accounts    (B) with a view to    (C) owing to    (D) in order to

_____ 3. (A) politician    (B) journalist    (C) investor    (D) media

_____ 4. (A) phenomenon    (B) mirror    (C) raisin    (D) scene

_____ 5. (A) even though    (B) as if    (C) now that    (D) in that

_____ 6. (A) would rather    (B) had better    (C) would like    (D) might as well

_____ 7. (A) glimpsing    (B) humiliating    (C) starving    (D) obtaining

_____ 8. (A) carriage    (B) blouse    (C) hobby    (D) fantasy

_____ 9. (A) helpful    (B) tragic    (C) comic    (D) minor

_____ 10. (A) melt    (B) lengthen    (C) cultivate    (D) subtract

完成日期：_____

實戰語錄

*Live and learn.*

*活到老，學到老。*

# I. Vocabulary

_____ 1. She didn't return my calls. I don't think she is _____ in helping us.

    (A) sincere     (B) ashamed     (C) dishonest     (D) dreadful

_____ 2. I cannot _____ his safety. He is old enough to be responsible for it.

    (A) prevent     (B) ignore     (C) flatter     (D) guarantee

_____ 3. You can _____ the screw by turning it counterclockwise.

    (A) lose     (B) lengthen     (C) loosen     (D) lessen

_____ 4. Joe's parents gave him such a small _____ that he had to earn extra money working in McDonald's.

    (A) celebration     (B) album     (C) allowance     (D) liberty

_____ 5. After dinner, I like to walk along the _____ of the sea with my husband.

    (A) shore     (B) route     (C) chore     (D) routine

_____ 6. Taiwan is very hot and _____ in summer.

    (A) humid     (B) bleak     (C) freezing     (D) mild

_____ 7. The boy played practical jokes on his classmates out of _____.

    (A) sympathy     (B) mischief     (C) curiosity     (D) passion

_____ 8. The economic depression has led to many small business' _____.

    (A) steadiness     (B) wildness     (C) blindness     (D) bankruptcy

_____ 9. Let's drink a _____ to the newly married couple.

    (A) report     (B) stroke     (C) boast     (D) toast

_____ 10. Some people cannot _____ one color from another. They are color-blind.

    (A) devise     (B) distinguish     (C) distribute     (D) discard

_____ 11. It is _____ for young children to be curious and keep asking questions about things around them.

    (A) peculiar     (B) unusual     (C) exceptional     (D) normal

_____ 12. The tennis championship is _____ live to countries around the world.

    (A) played     (B) programmed     (C) broadcast     (D) conveyed

_____ 13. He has not done the _____ for two weeks, and the dirty clothes are scattered around the room.

    (A) laundry     (B) laughter     (C) labor     (D) landing

_____ 14. Never achieve a terrific speed at the _____ of safety.

    (A) expansion     (B) expectation     (C) experience     (D) expense

_____ 15. Green trees will produce _____ during the day and help to clean the air we breathe.

(A) atmosphere     (B) vapor     (C) oxygen     (D) moisture

_____ 16. The child didn't swallow his food properly and started to _____.

(A) choke     (B) survive     (C) sneeze     (D) faint

_____ 17. She does exercise to keep _____.

(A) financial     (B) humble     (C) initial     (D) slim

_____ 18. A _____ of roadmen were repairing the road.

(A) gun     (B) gum     (C) gang     (D) grain

_____ 19. To have healthy babies, women should stop drinking and smoking during _____.

(A) frequency     (B) pregnancy     (C) bankruptcy     (D) accuracy

_____ 20. Do you think we should put the bookshelf in the _____?

(A) ceiling     (B) roof     (C) wall     (D) corner

## II. Idioms & Phrases

_____ 1. Don't always _____ me. It's unfair.

(A) pick on     (B) burst out     (C) bump into     (D) apply for

_____ 2. I must have _____ for I have the same symptoms as yours.

(A) complained about it        (B) dreamed of you

(C) get into your trouble        (D) caught your cold

_____ 3. I'll _____ as soon as I arrive in America.

(A) make an impression        (B) give you a ring

(C) take you in        (D) figure out

_____ 4. Ring the bell _____ emergency.

(A) in fear of        (B) in case of

(C) in harmony with        (D) in connection with

_____ 5. The old couple _____ in their son's achievements.

(A) took pride        (B) prided themselves

(C) were proud        (D) felt pride

_____ 6. The economic situation has _____ recently.

(A) brought home the bacon        (B) got into trouble

(C) acted on        (D) gone from bad to worse

_____ 7. The man in a wheelchair is too weak to _____ his feet.

(A) result in     (B) rise to     (C) run across     (D) run out of

_____ 8. She tiptoed quietly into the room _____ she might wake up the baby.

   (A) in that     (B) for fear that     (C) unless     (D) despite that

_____ 9. "Can I borrow your car?" "_____. You always make a mess in my car."

   (A) No problem     (B) I don't care

   (C) Absolutely not     (D) Only on certain conditions

_____ 10. She finally _____ a brilliant idea to double her income.

   (A) came up with     (B) came out     (C) came off     (D) came on

# III. Cloze Test

### Part A

Time is of essence at the workplace. In many large companies, workers have time cards that they must insert into time clocks. The clocks punch arrival and ___1___ times on employees' time cards so that wages can be ___2___. Many other places of employment use time sheets, on which employees are ___3___ to sign in and out at the beginning and end of a day's work.

In many employment sectors where quick and efficient performance is of the utmost importance, employees are ___4___ by computers. Telephone ___5___, for example, must assist a certain number of customers ___6___ minute. If the computerized record of their productivity shows below-average performance, they are given a ___7___ by their supervisors and are ___8___ that they must conform to the company's standard.

The emphasis ___9___ on time can be summed up in the ___10___, "Time is money." In some cases, just a few minutes may be worth millions of dollars.

_____ 1. (A) leave     (B) part     (C) departure     (D) away
_____ 2. (A) counted     (B) added     (C) computed     (D) calculated
_____ 3. (A) required     (B) wanted     (C) needless     (D) essential
_____ 4. (A) monitored     (B) motioned     (C) mentioned     (D) memorized
_____ 5. (A) mechanics     (B) engineers     (C) operators     (D) receivers
_____ 6. (A) by     (B) per     (C) for     (D) within
_____ 7. (A) threat     (B) warning     (C) suggestion     (D) punishment
_____ 8. (A) suggested     (B) advised     (C) recommended     (D) proposed
_____ 9. (A) lain     (B) placed     (C) planted     (D) added
_____ 10. (A) word     (B) line     (C) say     (D) proverb

### Part B

Heredity is not the only thing that ___1___ our color. Where we live and how we live after we were ___2___ are important too. For instance, our genes affect how fat or thin we are.

But our ____3____ depends mainly on how much we eat and how much ____4____ we take. ____5____, our skin color depends to a large ____6____ on how much sunshine we get.

There are three ____7____ to the question "Where does our color come from?" It comes from the genes we ____8____. It comes from the conditions in which we live. And it can come from a bottle of suntan ____9____ that we buy at the drugstore on the ____10____.

_____ 1. (A) wrinkles     (B) softens     (C) influences     (D) pollutes

_____ 2. (A) dressed     (B) born     (C) quarreled     (D) recognized

_____ 3. (A) weight     (B) height     (C) tribe     (D) age

_____ 4. (A) radar     (B) resource     (C) sympathy     (D) exercise

_____ 5. (A) For a while     (B) At a time     (C) On the way     (D) In the same way

_____ 6. (A) concept     (B) notion     (C) riddle     (D) extent

_____ 7. (A) odds     (B) accesses     (C) answers     (D) pioneers

_____ 8. (A) donate     (B) bury     (C) inherit     (D) sacrifice

_____ 9. (A) juice     (B) lotion     (C) vitamin     (D) insurance

_____ 10. (A) corner     (B) route     (C) temple     (D) welfare

完成日期：_____

挑戰語錄

*The pen is mightier than the sword.*
文勝於武。

## I. Vocabulary

_____ 1. The _____ of an English composition is different from that of a Chinese composition.

(A) exhibition     (B) fashion     (C) harmony     (D) structure

_____ 2. The old woman _____ over the death of her son.

(A) grieved     (B) believed     (C) relieved     (D) deceived

_____ 3. The ruler demanded absolute _____ from his subjects.

(A) precision     (B) similarity     (C) standard     (D) loyalty

_____ 4. This golf tournament is open to both _____ and professionals.

(A) agents     (B) amateurs     (C) publishers     (D) servants

_____ 5. I am not your _____. Don't order me to do these things.

(A) hero     (B) owner     (C) passenger     (D) slave

_____ 6. The island is sparsely _____. The population is only about 25,000.

(A) preserved     (B) deserted     (C) protected     (D) inhabited

_____ 7. This organization is meant to help those _____ children who suffer from domestic violence.

(A) accidental     (B) terrific     (C) miserable     (D) discouraged

_____ 8. They have _____ enough to pay the rent this month.

(A) barely     (B) properly     (C) rarely     (D) accidentally

_____ 9. Here comes an old man with _____ hair.

(A) slender     (B) silent     (C) sincere     (D) silver

_____ 10. She _____ her husband because he was on drugs and had no regular job.

(A) married     (B) proposed     (C) engaged     (D) divorced

_____ 11. I always keep pen and paper on hand so that I can take _____ whenever I need to.

(A) notes     (B) notice     (C) writings     (D) reports

_____ 12. The teacher was sued because he gave his student a(n) _____ beating.

(A) soft     (B) brutal     (C) urgent     (D) tender

_____ 13. I haven't heard from her _____ we graduated from high school.

(A) while     (B) if     (C) whenever     (D) since

_____ 14. He abandoned his family to pursue _____ and fortune.

(A) wealth     (B) health     (C) fame     (D) fancy

_____ 15. There are beautifully wrapped _____ lying around the Christmas tree.

    (A) baggage     (B) luggage     (C) packages     (D) passages

_____ 16. I'll sing the song and I'd like you all to join in the _____.

    (A) chorus     (B) orchestra     (C) symphony     (D) chamber

_____ 17. The weather was so hot that he _____ all over.

    (A) digested     (B) affected     (C) sweated     (D) floated

_____ 18. There is a wide _____ between their views.

    (A) hop     (B) gap     (C) tap     (D) sip

_____ 19. Before the refrigerator was invented, people used to _____ food by drying it in the sun or soaking it in salt.

    (A) reserve     (B) conserve     (C) preserve     (D) deserve

_____ 20. Singers performing Mozart's opera often wear historical _____.

    (A) ruins     (B) architecture     (C) hints     (D) costumes

## II. Idioms & Phrases

_____ 1. The airport was closed during the war, but it _____ now.

    (A) comes into use     (B) comes true     (C) comes along     (D) comes to an end

_____ 2. My English teacher _____ speaking. We practice speaking English hard in class.

    (A) interferes with         (B) catches a glimpse of

    (C) loses sight of         (D) puts emphasis on

_____ 3. The old scholar _____ last night. His funeral will be held next week.

    (A) passed out     (B) passed by     (C) passed through     (D) passed away

_____ 4. We must _____ between reckless spending and penny pitching.

    (A) keep the balance         (B) lose the balance

    (C) strike a balance         (D) upset the balance

_____ 5. He _____ losing his life to save the drowning boy.

    (A) took a risk of         (B) took a look at

    (C) took charge of         (D) took advantage of

_____ 6. The coffee is _____ that in quality. That's why it is cheaper.

    (A) senior to     (B) inferior to     (C) junior to     (D) prior to

_____ 7. "I wonder if you would like to go to the dance with me?" "Sorry. But may I _____? I happen to have an appointment with my dentist tonight."

    (A) take a walk     (B) go for nothing     (C) take a rain check     (D) lose my temper

_____ 8. According to the Greek mythology, Helen's beauty was _____.

    (A) for company                (B) for comparison

    (C) beyond comparison         (D) in bad company

_____ 9. I _____ seek the higher position without the support of voters.

    (A) was not suited to          (B) was urged not to

    (C) was not looking forward to     (D) was not devoted to

_____ 10. The poor couple tried hard to _____ .

    (A) make an error    (B) come into effect    (C) make ends meet    (D) drag their feet

# III. Cloze Test

## Part A

    It is generally agreed that the American system is in deep trouble. The problem lies not so much in our institutions as in our ___1___ . It is said that although most of us profess to believe in education, we ___2___ no value on intellectual activity. We Americans are a charitable and humane people: we have institutions ___3___ to every good cause from rescuing homeless cats to ___4___ World War III. But what have we done to promote the art of thinking? Certainly we ___5___ thought in our daily lives. Suppose a man were to say to his friends, "I'm not going to PTA tonight because I need some time to myself, some time to think." Such a man would be shunned by his neighbors; his family would ___6___ him. What if a teenager were to say, "___7___ going to the dance tonight, I need some time to think." His parents would immediately start looking in the Yellow Pages for a(n) ___8___ . We are all too much like Julius Caesar: we fear and ___9___ people who think too much. We believe that almost anything is ___10___ important than thinking.

_____ 1. (A) attitudes     (B) equipment     (C) graduation     (D) capability

_____ 2. (A) greet     (B) affect     (C) check     (D) place

_____ 3. (A) opposed     (B) devoted     (C) thankful     (D) weak

_____ 4. (A) encouraging     (B) urging     (C) preventing     (D) promoting

_____ 5. (A) look down upon            (B) feel sorry for

    (C) take care of            (D) make no room for

_____ 6. (A) be ashamed of     (B) be proud of     (C) be fond of     (D) be pleased with

_____ 7. (A) In spite of            (B) Instead of

    (C) At least            (D) As a matter of fact

_____ 8. (A) architect     (B) psychiatrist     (C) surgeon     (D) astronaut

_____ 9. (A) distrust     (B) welcome     (C) accept     (D) disapprove

_____ 10. (A) less     (B) much     (C) more     (D) even

Part B

The 1960s represented a ___1___ of great change in the United States of America. It was a period in which a frustrated African American population would finally get what was coming to them, ___2___. For centuries the progress of black people in America was ___3___ due to the extreme racism and ___4___. Largely under the leadership of a gentleman named Dr. Martin Luther King, African Americans were able to ___5___ racism not only in the American government, but also in the country's ___6___. Martin Luther King and all his followers ___7___ shaping a better and more stable America where black people would no longer have to ___8___ prejudice. The successful struggle of the African American population made ___9___ in the history of the world. Those who love equality and freedom ___10___ Martin Luther King and his followers a great of gratitude.

_____ 1. (A) decade     (B) debate     (C) debt     (D) defense

_____ 2. (A) just     (B) unjust     (C) justice     (D) injustice

_____ 3. (A) set up     (B) set back     (C) set out     (D) set forth

_____ 4. (A) prejudice     (B) conscience     (C) immigration     (D) industrialization

_____ 5. (A) expose     (B) propose     (C) pose     (D) pause

_____ 6. (A) corners     (B) courses     (C) currents     (D) courts

_____ 7. (A) had their hearts set on     (B) put their feet in their mouths

        (C) had their mouths shut for     (D) turned up their noses at

_____ 8. (A) cope with     (B) confess to     (C) contribute to     (D) contrast with

_____ 9. (A) a slight error     (B) a hasty conclusion

        (C) an enormous mark     (D) no big deal

_____ 10. (A) draw     (B) tow     (C) own     (D) owe

完成日期：_____

戰語錄

*When one door shuts another opens.*
天無絕人之路（柳暗花明又一村）。

## I. Vocabulary

_____ 1. A snake-charmer is playing his pipe in the town _____. Do you want to see it?

    (A) yard       (B) square       (C) horizon       (D) balcony

_____ 2. I expressed my sincere _____ to him for his valuable instruction.

    (A) attitude       (B) gratitude       (C) altitude       (D) magnitude

_____ 3. Passengers must keep their _____ either under their seats or in the overhead compartments.

    (A) luggage       (B) account       (C) fragment       (D) passage

_____ 4. _____, she stood and stared while the police broke into her house.

    (A) Disappointed     (B) Delighted     (C) Twisted     (D) Amazed

_____ 5. Many _____ came here to offer their help selflessly.

    (A) statues       (B) robots       (C) volunteers       (D) scarecrows

_____ 6. Keep me _____ of the changes in the stock prices.

    (A) insured       (B) exposed       (C) informed       (D) assured

_____ 7. It is unkind of you to laugh at other people's _____.

    (A) absence       (B) humor       (C) misfortune       (D) success

_____ 8. This shirt is half-price, a real _____.

    (A) expense       (B) cost       (C) entertainment     (D) bargain

_____ 9. I saw him several minutes ago. He must be _____ in the building.

    (A) somewhere     (B) somewhat     (C) somehow     (D) sometimes

_____ 10. The Romans once _____ Europe. They had power over it.

    (A) dominated     (B) ruined       (C) rebuilt       (D) established

_____ 11. Milk and eggs are considered _____ foods, which can provide you with energy you need for work.

    (A) polishing     (B) publishing     (C) diminishing     (D) nourishing

_____ 12. The living cost is much higher these days, so I find it hard to live within _____.

    (A) budget       (B) surroundings     (C) margins       (D) cost

_____ 13. Basically, the article can be _____ in three sentences.

    (A) surrounded     (B) succeeded     (C) summarized     (D) supported

_____ 14. I thought he was my friend but his friendship was _____.

    (A) false       (B) identical       (C) plastic       (D) concrete

_____ 15. The gardener is trimming the bushes with a huge _____ of scissors.

      (A) piece        (B) couple        (C) pair        (D) double

_____ 16. The bad news quickly _____ around the whole town.

      (A) surrounded        (B) extended        (C) circulated        (D) arrived

_____ 17. The firefighters tried hard to stop the fire from _____ .

      (A) elimination        (B) extinction        (C) devotion        (D) spreading

_____ 18. Tell me _____ where it is.

      (A) sharply        (B) exactly        (C) keenly        (D) extremely

_____ 19. With the final examination coming, the students are under great _____ to finish studying all these books.

      (A) force        (B) power        (C) pressure        (D) relief

_____ 20. The smoke of cigarettes always makes me _____ .

      (A) yawn        (B) hiccup        (C) cough        (D) laugh

## II. Idioms & Phrases

_____ 1. To pay off his debt, he had to _____ his car.

      (A) separate with        (B) depart from        (C) part with        (D) cut off from

_____ 2. He committed a serious crime and spent most of his life _____ .

      (A) under control              (B) behind bars

      (C) within reach              (D) beating about the bush

_____ 3. She was _____ her purse in the park this morning.

      (A) sick of        (B) robbed of        (C) bound for        (D) cut out for

_____ 4. The inhabitants were _____ malaria and one of them was dying.

      (A) pleased with        (B) infected with        (C) jam-packed with     (D) covered with

_____ 5. He goes for a walk every day on the beach _____ .

      (A) happily ever after   (B) far ahead        (C) in time        (D) rain or shine

_____ 6. If you want to pass the exam, you'll have to _____ your listening abilities.

      (A) concentrate on   (B) congratulate on    (C) prevent from     (D) protest against

_____ 7. They _____ of the dispute. The driver needed to pay the victim of the car accident 50,000 dollars.

      (A) came in first place          (B) took their turns

      (C) were robbed               (D) came to a settlement

_____ 8. It's a pity that more and more young people are _____ .

      (A) letting go of drugs        (B) on drugs

      (C) prescribing drugs        (D) opposed to drugs

_____ 9. His plan is only _____ . It can never be put into practice.

(A) a pain in the neck        (B) a pie in the sky

(C) an apple in the eye        (D) a frog in the throat

_____ 10. The film _____ a true story of a gold miner in the 19ᵗʰ century.

(A) is bound for     (B) is obliged to     (C) is up to     (D) is based on

# III. Cloze Test

**Part A**

Stop all the clocks, cut off the telephone,

___1___ the dog from barking with a juicy bone,

Silence the ___2___ and with muffled drum

Bring out the coffin, let the mourners come.


Let aeroplanes circle moaning overhead

Scribbling on the sky the ___3___ *He Is Dead*,

Put crêpe bows ___4___ the white necks of the public doves,

Let the traffic ___5___ wear black cotton gloves.


He was my North, my South, my East and West,

My working week and my Sunday ___6___,

My noon, my ___7___, my talk, my song;

I thought that love would ___8___ forever; I was wrong.


The stars are not wanted now; ___9___ every one;

Pack up the ___10___ and dismantle the sun;

Pour away the ocean and sweep up the wood;

For nothing now can ever come to any good.

(Funeral Blues W.H. Auden)

| | | | | |
|---|---|---|---|---|
| _____ 1. | (A) Adapt | (B) Borrow | (C) Isolate | (D) Prevent |
| _____ 2. | (A) pianos | (B) ceiling | (C) family | (D) flame |
| _____ 3. | (A) advice | (B) message | (C) danger | (D) report |
| _____ 4. | (A) in | (B) with | (C) around | (D) off |
| _____ 5. | (A) signs | (B) movements | (C) policemen | (D) advances |
| _____ 6. | (A) morning | (B) mass | (C) party | (D) rest |
| _____ 7. | (A) midnight | (B) love | (C) life | (D) friend |
| _____ 8. | (A) stop | (B) end | (C) have | (D) last |

_____ 9. (A) light up      (B) put out      (C) turn on      (D) set up

_____ 10. (A) suitcase      (B) package      (C) moon      (D) clothes

### Part B

I remember attending the marriage of my friend Josh and his beautiful ____1____ Kelly. The wedding ____2____ in a pristine church filled with people ____3____. It was a very holy and sentimental time. In the back room, I noticed that Josh was filled with anxiety. He looked as if he could not deal with the pressure of ____4____. He roamed the halls of the church ____5____ about how unpredictable marriage could be. He kept telling me that many marriages seem stable at first, but overnight they ____6____ and end up in divorce. I reminded Josh of ____7____ he had his eye on Kelly and what a great chemistry they had together. It's normal for marriages to go through ups and downs, so one ____8____ about what might happen in the future. I told Josh that he had such ____9____ to be marrying an amazing woman like Kelly and that they would be happy for the rest of their lives together. It is now fifty years later and I am on my way to what will be a great ____10____ party.

_____ 1. (A) bride      (B) maid      (C) housekeeper      (D) secretary

_____ 2. (A) hit upon      (B) took place      (C) held on      (D) occurred to

_____ 3. (A) dressed in dazzling outfits      (B) naked

     (C) disguised as clowns      (D) in rags

_____ 4. (A) putting down      (B) tearing down      (C) burning down      (D) settling down

_____ 5. (A) frustrating      (B) frustrated      (C) frustrate      (D) frustratingly

_____ 6. (A) come apart      (B) fall apart      (C) tell apart      (D) set apart

_____ 7. (A) why on earth      (B) how long      (C) what in the world (D) whoever

_____ 8. (A) cannot jump to conclusions      (B) cannot but wonder

     (C) had better talk      (D) is supposed to be curious

_____ 9. (A) great wealth      (B) big muscles      (C) good fortune      (D) hard luck

_____ 10. (A) funeral      (B) convention      (C) anniversary      (D) farewell

完成日期：＿＿＿＿＿＿＿

**實戰語錄**

_A stitch in time saves nine._

小洞不補，大來吃苦。

## I. Vocabulary

_____ 1. Your jacket is _____ to mine. They are both dark blue in color.

    (A) similar     (B) familiar     (C) related     (D) connected

_____ 2. To live a long and healthy life, you must avoid _____ food.

    (A) nutritious     (B) fresh     (C) greasy     (D) frozen

_____ 3. The mother kept singing _____ until her baby fell asleep.

    (A) symphonies     (B) melodies     (C) summaries     (D) lullabies

_____ 4. Quick, call the _____. I think the man has had a heart attack.

    (A) ambulance     (B) airport     (C) earphone     (D) individual

_____ 5. She was the only _____ of the shipwreck. The other people were killed.

    (A) victim     (B) survivor     (C) volunteer     (D) captain

_____ 6. Jane thinks in all _____ that her beauty will get everything for her.

    (A) courtesy     (B) innocence     (C) manners     (D) temper

_____ 7. He was _____ by bad company and fell into a life of drinking and gambling.

    (A) misled     (B) polluted     (C) sheltered     (D) guided

_____ 8. Shyness is one of the biggest _____ to making friends.

    (A) barriers     (B) emotions     (C) feelings     (D) excitements

_____ 9. The best way to get a man's heart is through his _____. Girls, learn to cook well.

    (A) nose     (B) lung     (C) liver     (D) stomach

_____ 10. He has no _____ talent. He is poor at acting.

    (A) poetic     (B) romantic     (C) dramatic     (D) critic

_____ 11. He is a liberal person and is always open-minded to any _____ ideas.

    (A) mystery     (B) fiction     (C) novel     (D) romance

_____ 12. Without a ladder, I am unable to change the _____.

    (A) floor     (B) bulb     (C) carpet     (D) furniture

_____ 13. The boat was going to _____, so the passengers put on their lifejackets quickly.

    (A) kick     (B) sink     (C) trick     (D) wink

_____ 14. The little boy often _____ himself as a great scientist.

    (A) leads     (B) links     (C) fancies     (D) confuses

_____ 15. All the little animals fled in _____ when they saw the lion approaching.

    (A) happiness     (B) sadness     (C) grief     (D) panic

_____ 16. When I was little, I loved watching clowns and animals performing in a _____.

    (A) temple         (B) cliff         (C) library         (D) circus

_____ 17. But for your _____, I would fall down and get hurt.

    (A) warning         (B) compliment         (C) extension         (D) gratitude

_____ 18. Some doctors _____ upon a diet which contains only vegetables.

    (A) oppose         (B) rebel         (C) disapprove         (D) frown

_____ 19. He is determined and nothing can _____ him from achieving his goal.

    (A) cease         (B) pause         (C) prevent         (D) forbid

_____ 20. What you wear must _____ to your self-image.

    (A) reply         (B) correspond         (C) devote         (D) contribute

## II. Idioms & Phrases

_____ 1. I would like to have my whiskey _____. It won't be so strong.

    (A) on purpose         (B) on the rocks         (C) on the job         (D) on the whole

_____ 2. Keep me _____ the latest information.

    (A) convinced of         (B) informed of         (C) assured of         (D) persuaded of

_____ 3. I cannot _____ his rude behavior any more.

    (A) put up with         (B) be absent from     (C) come across         (D) put on

_____ 4. He was knocked down by a car and was sent to hospital _____.

    (A) at a time         (B) ahead of time     (C) from time to time  (D) in no time

_____ 5. A warning sign, saying "No swimming," is _____ by the lake.

    (A) sped up         (B) set up         (C) switched off         (D) rolled up

_____ 6. You must be careful or you may _____ getting hurt.

    (A) end up         (B) send up         (C) get up         (D) turn up

_____ 7. The scientists _____ of the movements of the earth.

    (A) keep a record     (B) hold a record     (C) set up a record     (D) break a record

_____ 8. It was so hot that I _____ sweat.

    (A) was bathed in                 (B) was associated with

    (C) involved with                 (D) couldn't help

_____ 9. The teacher _____ to see who was absent.

    (A) crossed her fingers         (B) called it a day

    (C) called a roll                (D) called students down

_____ 10. _____ he saw the policeman, he ran away.

    (A) The instant         (B) The reason         (C) No sooner         (D) No longer

## III. Cloze Test

### Part A

In the United States the cost of living has been steadily rising for the past few decades. Food prices, clothing costs, housing expenses, and tuition fees are constantly getting ___1___. Partly because of financial need, and partly because of career choices for personal ___2___, mothers have been leaving the ___3___ role of full-time homemaker. Increasingly they have been taking ___4___ jobs outside the home.

Making such a(n) ___5___ role change affects the entire family, especially the children. Some ___6___ are obvious. For example, dinner time is at a later hour. The emotion impact, ___7___, can be more subtle. Mothers leave home in the morning, feeling ___8___ because they will not be home when their children return from school. They suppress their guilt since they believe that their working will ___9___ everyone in the long run. The income will ___10___ the family to save for college tuition, take an extended vacation, buy a new car, and so on.

| | | | |
|---|---|---|---|
| _____ 1. (A) higher and higher | | (B) lower and lower | |
| (C) faster and faster | | (D) slower and slower | |
| _____ 2. (A) misfortune | (B) fulfillment | (C) admiration | (D) distinction |
| _____ 3. (A) defensive | (B) flexible | (C) traditional | (D) acceptable |
| _____ 4. (A) sensitive | (B) miserable | (C) salaried | (D) voluntary |
| _____ 5. (A) indifferent | (B) significant | (C) common | (D) easy |
| _____ 6. (A) achievements | (B) ingredients | (C) consequences | (D) organizations |
| _____ 7. (A) on the other hand | (B) on the contrary | (C) for one thing | (D) as a result |
| _____ 8. (A) guilty | (B) greasy | (C) greedy | (D) grateful |
| _____ 9. (A) believe | (B) belong | (C) bargain | (D) benefit |
| _____ 10. (A) enclose | (B) enable | (C) encounter | (D) endanger |

### Part B

In the mid-1980's a Canadian track and field ___1___ named Ben Johnson held the title as the world's fastest man. In the 100-meter dash he ___2___ the record time and was considered a(n) ___3___ figure throughout the country of Canada. However, in the 1988 Olympic Games, after winning the gold ___4___, Ben Johnson was disqualified from the ___5___ for illegally using steroids. ___6___ a giant in the world of track and field, Johnson soon became the ___7___ of ridicule as his image was destroyed. He was considered to be a ___8___ to his country and ___9___ suffered countless humiliations in the press. Ben Johnson tried to convince the world that he was ___10___ but nobody would believe him.

_____ 1. (A) athlete     (B) amateur     (C) referee     (D) coach

_____ 2. (A) is held     (B) holds     (C) held     (D) was held

_____ 3. (A) imaginary     (B) mysterious     (C) heroic     (D) fictitious

_____ 4. (A) metal     (B) medal     (C) middle     (D) meter

_____ 5. (A) meet     (B) court     (C) ring     (D) location

_____ 6. (A) Once     (B) But for     (C) Provided     (D) In case

_____ 7. (A) tack     (B) tablet     (C) task     (D) target

_____ 8. (A) jewel     (B) pride     (C) professional     (D) shame

_____ 9. (A) by contrast     (B) as a result     (C) nevertheless     (D) by and large

_____ 10. (A) sensible     (B) accidental     (C) innocent     (D) efficient

完成日期：—————————

 戰語錄

*While there is life there is hope.*
留得青山在，不怕沒柴燒。

信心指數
☆☆☆☆☆

## I. Vocabulary

_____ 1. The workers on the night _____ work from midnight to the early morning.

(A) manners      (B) surroundings      (C) condition      (D) shift

_____ 2. You cannot park your car in this area, which is reserved for the _____.

(A) handicapped      (B) injured      (C) dying      (D) genius

_____ 3. Ever since he made a fortune in business, he has been able to afford a life o f _____.

(A) accuracy      (B) luxury      (C) frequency      (D) majority

_____ 4. After _____ the situation, we had a clear idea about what we should do next.

(A) reflecting      (B) concluding      (C) analyzing      (D) nourishing

_____ 5. He _____ his shoes before he goes to sleep every night.

(A) shoots      (B) shocks      (C) shuts      (D) shines

_____ 6. I always get my _____ from the poems by Robert Frost.

(A) insistence      (B) inspection      (C) inspiration      (D) instruction

_____ 7. When they came home, they found the house had been broken into and all the valuables were _____.

(A) missing      (B) losing      (C) stealing      (D) vanishing

_____ 8. After she finished cleaning the mop, she _____ the water over the lawn.

(A) spilled      (B) spoiled      (C) poured      (D) spit

_____ 9. He works very hard. He has the _____ to succeed.

(A) courage      (B) taste      (C) drive      (D) grace

_____ 10. There are still worries about the negative influences a _____ power plant may have on the environment.

(A) nuisance      (B) nuclear      (C) nutritious      (D) numerous

_____ 11. The townspeople held a _____ in honor of the baseball team that had just won the championship.

(A) march      (B) hiking      (C) parade      (D) protest

_____ 12. I bought a _____ of flowers at the market.

(A) bucket      (B) barrel      (C) bottle      (D) bunch

_____ 13. The books in the library are _____ according to subject.

(A) canceled      (B) classified      (C) formed      (D) guessed

_____ 14. She wants to keep herself up-to-date and often reads magazines about the _____

fashion.

    (A) last             (B) latest            (C) later            (D) latter

_____ 15. He does everything in his own _____. He never follows what others do.

    (A) image           (B) fashion         (C) range           (D) kingdom

_____ 16. I have forgotten what we talked about in the _____ conversation. Can you help me refresh my memory?

    (A) before          (B) previous       (C) prior            (D) front

_____ 17. People should have _____ to stand up for their beliefs.

    (A) hesitation      (B) creativity      (C) courage       (D) gratitude

_____ 18. She made every _____ to give her children better education. She worked hard to afford their tuition.

    (A) sacrifice       (B) current        (C) energy        (D) frustration

_____ 19. Whenever he feels depressed, he goes to the country and stays in a _____ in the woods.

    (A) defeat         (B) retreat        (C) repeat         (D) threat

_____ 20. A trademark creates an image for a product and can be a powerful _____.

    (A) device         (B) supply         (C) topic          (D) sympathy

## II. Idioms & Phrases

_____ 1. Air pollution _____ a high percentage of the lung cancer cases.

    (A) results in     (B) results from    (C) is due to     (D) is caused by

_____ 2. I missed the bus this morning and _____ I was late to school.

    (A) in consequence  (B) in doubt      (C) in surprise     (D) in anger

_____ 3. Children _____ firecrackers during the Chinese New Year holidays.

    (A) play tricks on  (B) set aside      (C) set off       (D) run over

_____ 4. It rained five days_____ and many places were flooded.

    (A) at loose ends   (B) end to end    (C) no end       (D) on end

_____ 5. Five minutes after the firemen came, the fire was _____.

    (A) put on        (B) put out       (C) put off      (D) put forward

_____ 6. _____ the storm, the boat was tipped over.

    (A) Regardless of  (B) Becoming of  (C) Judging from  (D) Because of

_____ 7. The kind girl _____ the pregnant woman on the bus.

    (A) made room for              (B) made a difference in

    (C) made her way to            (D) made fun of

_____ 8. His snores _____ my sleep. The disturbance drove me crazy.

(A) interfered with    (B) bathed with    (C) crowded with    (D) impressed with

_____ 9. I have to _____ my French before I go on a trip to Paris.

     (A) pass by      (B) pick out      (C) polish up      (D) put up

_____ 10. Most people in the country _____ him as the best President they have ever had.

     (A) look up      (B) think of      (C) take in      (D) let on

## III. Cloze Test

### Part A

You are standing in the cereal aisle at the ___1___ store, searching for your favorite ___2___. Suddenly, you catch a whiff of chocolate-chip cookies. Your mouth begins to water. You forget about cereal and ___3___ the bakery section.

Guess what? You just walked into an odor ___4___! The yummy smell was fake. The odor was cooked up by scientists in a lab, then ___5___ by the store's owners to lure you to the bakery section.

_____ 1. (A) drug      (B) department      (C) grocery      (D) hardware

_____ 2. (A) bowl      (B) guarantee      (C) cafeteria      (D) brand

_____ 3. (A) head for      (B) take for      (C) long for      (D) ask for

_____ 4. (A) appetite      (B) trap      (C) empire      (D) export

_____ 5. (A) sealed      (B) appointed      (C) sworn      (D) spread

### Part B

Last summer an international soccer competition in Belgium ___1___ into violence as English soccer fans caused great damage to numerous Belgian cities. The English are hooked on soccer and are known to be passionate soccer fans; however, their recent behavior has been totally ___2___. Their actions have done much to ___3___ the spirit and charm of the sport. The international soccer community has taken this issue very ___4___ and has urged the English government to do something about its country's soccer fans. The English government regrets the behavior of its citizens and as a result has introduced a ___5___ that would ban violent fans from leaving England to attend international soccer games.

_____ 1. (A) explored      (B) exploded      (C) expanded      (D) expected

_____ 2. (A) accepted      (B) acceptable      (C) unacceptable      (D) unacceptably

_____ 3. (A) awaken      (B) recover      (C) ruin      (D) raise

_____ 4. (A) easy      (B) well      (C) lightly      (D) seriously

_____ 5. (A) privilege      (B) privacy      (C) product      (D) proposal

### Part C

R
O
U
N
D

2
1

Consumerism simply means buying. Its pattern in Britain, as well as in many other countries, has changed a lot in the last 20 years. People ___1___ go to several shops to buy their daily goods. They went to one shop to buy meat, another to buy fish and ___2___ another to buy vegetables. Salt, sugar, and canned food came from a ___3___; toothpaste, cosmetics and medicines from a ___4___. These days, people usually do their shopping in a supermarket. There, under one ___5___, they can buy all the goods they want.

In the food shops, the goods are weighed on ___6___ and put into a paper bag. Sometimes they were thrown ___7___ into a shopping bag. Meat and fish must have been ___8___ in special paper. All the fruits in the supermarkets are the same in size and color. They look this way because they have been treated with chemicals to ___9___ its growth. People are wondering if they want to eat such fruit at the ___10___ of taking in all these chemicals.

_____ 1. (A) get used to    (B) used to    (C) are used to    (D) are used for

_____ 2. (A) still    (B) ever    (C) while    (D) after

_____ 3. (A) factory    (B) museum    (C) grocery    (D) skyscraper

_____ 4. (A) bakery    (B) restaurant    (C) apartment    (D) drugstore

_____ 5. (A) light    (B) corner    (C) roof    (D) brick

_____ 6. (A) cranes    (B) cameras    (C) scales    (D) servants

_____ 7. (A) indirectly    (B) individually    (C) straight    (D) additionally

_____ 8. (A) wrapped    (B) equipped    (C) designed    (D) tied

_____ 9. (A) injure    (B) preserve    (C) encourage    (D) regulate

_____ 10. (A) risk    (B) hope    (C) proposal    (D) sight

完成日期：_____

實戰語錄

*Better late than never.*
*不怕慢，只怕站。*

信心指數
☆☆☆☆☆

# I. Vocabulary

_____ 1. She doesn't want to get married. She wants to remain _____ .

(A) steady     (B) firm     (C) single     (D) isolated

_____ 2. The drama consists of ordinary _____ of daily life.

(A) incidents     (B) tragedies     (C) celebrations     (D) disasters

_____ 3. It is ironical that human beings have invented modern _____ to make life easier, but end up living a much busier life.

(A) behavior     (B) machinery     (C) household     (D) photography

_____ 4. People have been using fire since _____ times.

(A) ancient     (B) angel     (C) modern     (D) romantic

_____ 5. He _____ the thief by the arm and took him to the police station.

(A) adopted     (B) displayed     (C) seized     (D) hushed

_____ 6. The woman _____ herself in a river for she found life was not worth living.

(A) drummed     (B) drowned     (C) drunk     (D) drained

_____ 7. He believes that his _____ of life is to help the poor people.

(A) mission     (B) permission     (C) impression     (D) admission

_____ 8. The crane used its _____ to catch fish.

(A) hand     (B) leg     (C) arm     (D) beak

_____ 9. At the end of every month, my money left is _____ .

(A) scary     (B) severe     (C) secure     (D) scarce

_____ 10. Traffic was _____ for hours by accident.

(A) halted     (B) conducted     (C) destroyed     (D) improved

_____ 11. The complaints from the citizens are too _____ to ignore, so the government has to take actions to solve the problem.

(A) plenty     (B) countless     (C) numerous     (D) abundant

_____ 12. Buying a house usually places a big financial _____ on young couples.

(A) bundle     (B) bullet     (C) burden     (D) bureau

_____ 13. The missing boy was found _____ the streets alone.

(A) wondering     (B) winding     (C) wrecking     (D) wandering

_____ 14. The scandal was _____ to his reputation.

(A) fearful     (B) fantastic     (C) favorite     (D) fatal

_____ 15. It is required by the law that all the _____ in a car must fasten their seat belts.

(A) companions     (B) passengers     (C) interpreters     (D) headquarters

_____ 16. Keep your fingers away from the crab's _____ when you pick it up.

(A) clay            (B) claps            (C) claws            (D) clashes

_____ 17. The tools the miners are using are still _____, so it is hard to increase their production.

(A) advanced     (B) progressive     (C) primitive     (D) original

_____ 18. The chicken looks so tasty that I cannot _____ the temptation of getting a bite.

(A) consist       (B) insist         (C) resist         (D) persist

_____ 19. You might get along better with your parents if you show them some _____.

(A) courtesy     (B) tension     (C) function     (D) participation

_____ 20. The cake is so _____ that I'd like to have one more piece.

(A) delicious     (B) striking     (C) spicy     (D) diverse

## II. Idioms & Phrases

_____ 1. The volunteers are _____ offer their help after the earthquake.

(A) devoted to                (B) looking forward to

(C) opposed to              (D) willing to

_____ 2. I enjoyed myself _____ in the party.

(A) to the full     (B) in full bloom     (C) at full speed     (D) in full

_____ 3. They are going to _____ the old house and build a new office building.

(A) pull up     (B) pull down     (C) pull in     (D) pull over

_____ 4. Thank you for your advice. I'll bear it _____.

(A) at hand     (B) over the counter     (C) in mind     (D) at large

_____ 5. Life is not likely to be _____. There is something unpleasant always.

(A) in the dark     (B) a bed of roses     (C) on the job     (D) a top priority

_____ 6. The following sentences must be _____ Chinese.

(A) put into     (B) moved into     (C) made into     (D) transformed into

_____ 7. No matter how busy he is, he has never _____ his concern for his wife and children.

(A) given priority to    (B) given thought to    (C) lost sight of    (D) laid emphasis on

_____ 8. I _____ my present job. I don't want to change to another one.

(A) am surprised at             (B) am concerned with

(C) am discouraged from       (D) am content with

_____ 9. The road is 10 meters _____.

(A) in season     (B) in width     (C) in vain     (D) in a hurry

_____ 10. I have to withdraw some money from the bank, mail a letter in the post office, and _____ some errands.

     (A) catch up       (B) make up       (C) run       (D) submit

# III. Cloze Test

**Part A**

    It is easy to understand the greenhouse effect by thinking of the greenhouse in a garden. If you have one, go and sit in it on a sunny day. The sun is ____1____ through the glass. It is warming up the air, warming up the earth and the plants that grow there. The glass is doing two things. It is letting the sunshine in and preventing much of the warmth from ____2____. So the greenhouse is a heat ____3____. Now imagine. The Earth is inside a kind of greenhouse: the atmosphere around it is the glass. Atmosphere is ____4____ to all living things: if the Earth suddenly loses it, the Earth will be as cold and lifeless as the moon. But we have a problem now. Our atmosphere is changing. We are polluting it with chemicals in the ____5____ of gases. You can't see the gases as they go up into the atmosphere, but they are one of the worst ____6____ facing the environment. The most important greenhouse gas is carbon dioxide. Humans ____7____ it when we breathe out, but there is nothing we can do about that! Its ____8____ source is the burning of fossil fuels and wood. There are other gases such as nitrogen dioxide and CFCs. These gases are building up in the atmosphere. And too little of the sun's heat is ____9____ to escape into space. The ____10____ of the earth is increasingly higher and higher.

_____ 1. (A) shifting       (B) shining       (C) sheltering       (D) shaping

_____ 2. (A) escaping       (B) appearing       (C) approaching       (D) occurring

_____ 3. (A) treat       (B) trap       (C) tool       (D) tray

_____ 4. (A) efficient       (B) essential       (C) expressive       (D) effective

_____ 5. (A) shape       (B) form       (C) shade       (D) foam

_____ 6. (A) threats       (B) chances       (C) theories       (D) experiments

_____ 7. (A) swallow       (B) reject       (C) propose       (D) produce

_____ 8. (A) main       (B) maid       (C) mean       (D) merry

_____ 9. (A) ordered       (B) discouraged       (C) allowed       (D) disapproved

_____ 10. (A) weight       (B) climate       (C) landscape       (D) temperature

**Part B**

    A good suggestion for consumers is to buy generic items ____1____ famous brands. Generic items in supermarkets ____2____ plain packages. These products are cheaper because ____3____ don't spend much money on packaging or advertising. The quality, however, is usually

_____4_____ to the quality of well-known name brands. _____5_____, when buying clothes, you can often find high quality and _____6_____ prices in brands that are not famous. Shopping in _____7_____ clothing stores can also help you save a lot of money. _____8_____ these stores aren't very attractive, and they usually don't have individual _____9_____ rooms, the prices are low, and you can often find the same famous brands that you find in _____10_____ department stores.

_____ 1. (A) as well as     (B) instead of     (C) due to     (D) were it not for

_____ 2. (A) come in     (B) come out     (C) come off     (D) come on

_____ 3. (A) consumers     (B) passengers     (C) manufacturers     (D) creators

_____ 4. (A) identical     (B) identity     (C) identified     (D) identification

_____ 5. (A) In a sense     (B) At any rate     (C) By any means     (D) In the same way

_____ 6. (A) cheap     (B) expensive     (C) low     (D) high

_____ 7. (A) dismissed     (B) discount     (C) disgusting     (D) distinguished

_____ 8. (A) As     (B) Since     (C) Although     (D) If

_____ 9. (A) dresser     (B) dressed     (C) dressing     (D) dressy

_____ 10. (A) high price     (B) high-priced     (C) low price     (D) low-priced

完成日期：_____

實戰語錄

*Never say die.*

絕不氣餒。

# I. Vocabulary

_____ 1. "Emphasis" has three _____ .

(A) intonations     (B) stories     (C) directions     (D) syllables

_____ 2. Many local residents gathered in the town _____ to talk face-to-face with the mayor.

(A) hall     (B) toll     (C) doll     (D) fall

_____ 3. She seems to possess such a _____ power that all the boys in town are attracted to her.

(A) deserted     (B) usual     (C) horrible     (D) magical

_____ 4. I don't want to miss the _____ musical festival. After all, it is held only once a year.

(A) private     (B) annual     (C) slender     (D) cable

_____ 5. The fruit is _____ enough for us to pick.

(A) rare     (B) destroyed     (C) greasy     (D) ripe

_____ 6. Taiwan is developing into an _____ nation.

(A) industrious     (B) industry     (C) industrialize     (D) industrial

_____ 7. Some people in the U.S. live in _____ homes, which can be moved from place to place.

(A) concrete     (B) mobile     (C) permanent     (D) ancient

_____ 8. We could just see the path in the weak _____ of a flashlight.

(A) bean     (B) bead     (C) beam     (D) battle

_____ 9. Miss Green was _____ of her purse in the park this morning. Her loss included 5 thousand dollars and 2 credit cards.

(A) identified     (B) distinguished     (C) suspected     (D) robbed

_____ 10. He was struck _____ with horror. His incapability of speaking remained for several minutes.

(A) dumb     (B) blind     (C) deaf     (D) diseased

_____ 11. Do you think it good for students to be absolutely _____ without making any objections in any case?

(A) innocent     (B) industrious     (C) obedient     (D) sincere

_____ 12. On entering my room, I undid the _____ on my shirt.

(A) buttons     (B) collar     (C) sleeves     (D) pocket

_____ 13. Who can live on a _____ as small as he gets?

    (A) furniture       (B) salary       (C) hardware       (D) identity

_____ 14. Fifty votes were in _____ of the bill and three were against it.

    (A) expression     (B) favor       (C) fever       (D) itch

_____ 15. The girl never tells what she likes or dislikes and only _____ takes whatever is offered.

    (A) passively     (B) positively     (C) actively     (D) earnestly

_____ 16. Richard has a(n) _____ plan for getting us out of our difficulties.

    (A) intelligent     (B) stupid     (C) dull       (D) clever

_____ 17. The principle reason for _____ humans with machines is to cut the cost of production.

    (A) substituting     (B) replacing     (C) offending     (D) removing

_____ 18. The mother rocked the _____ gently to calm her baby down.

    (A) crack       (B) crane       (C) crayon       (D) cradle

_____ 19. We were asked to _____ the play over and over again until our performance was perfect.

    (A) resign       (B) resolve     (C) recognize     (D) rehearse

_____ 20. It's raining outside. Why don't we have pizza _____ for dinner tonight?

    (A) demonstrated     (B) depressed     (C) deprived     (D) delivered

## II. Idioms & Phrases

_____ 1. I hate all this argument. I hope we can settle the dispute _____.

    (A) now and then   (B) now or never   (C) once more     (D) once and for all

_____ 2. When I got home, I was annoyed to discover that I had _____ my purse on the bus.

    (A) picked up     (B) left behind     (C) taken away     (D) built up

_____ 3. Don't _____ him. He is a hopeless fellow.

    (A) waste your breath on       (B) be independent of

    (C) make progress in          (D) go without

_____ 4. He was sent to prison because he was _____ the robbery.

    (A) involved in     (B) invested in     (C) ironed out     (D) impressed with

_____ 5. They have encountered _____ difficulty when they are working on the project.

    (A) a great deal of   (B) a lot       (C) a good sum     (D) hardly many

_____ 6. "Didn't you find the film exciting?" "_____, I fell asleep most of the time."

    (A) On the contrary   (B) In conclusion   (C) In brief     (D) In short

_____ 7. I have _____ too much weight so that the dress is too small for me.

    (A) put up with     (B) put off     (C) put on     (D) put away

_____ 8. He _____ running. He is the fastest runner in his class.

    (A) excels in     (B) finds fault with     (C) is fed up with     (D) is keen to

_____ 9. It is not nice of you to _____. After all, he is your classmate.

    (A) call his name              (B) call him by name

    (C) call him names            (D) call his last name

_____ 10. Let's _____ as monsters at the Halloween party.

    (A) make believe     (B) dress up     (C) believe in     (D) account for

# III. Cloze Test

**Part A**

There are five and a half billion people living on our planet. Each one of us interacts with only a very small ____1____ of the whole group; nevertheless, it would be possible to know thousands of people. In fact, however, we tend to form close relationships with quite a ____2____ number of individuals. During the last half of this century, social psychologists have been actively ____3____ to identify the basis we each use to ____4____ our social world to a manageable number of acquaintances—and to determine what ____5____ lead us to like some of the individuals and dislike others.

_____ 1. (A) information     (B) percentage     (C) proposal     (D) identification

_____ 2. (A) endless     (B) vast     (C) total     (D) limited

_____ 3. (A) opposed     (B) attempting     (C) urged     (D) devoted

_____ 4. (A) narrow     (B) strengthen     (C) widen     (D) deepen

_____ 5. (A) behaviors     (B) facilities     (C) figures     (D) factors

**Part B**

Many people are convinced that aliens visit us regularly. They say that the American government knows this but is ____1____ it up. In the last few years, thousands of Americans say they have been abducted by aliens. ____2____, there is so much ____3____ knowledge about aliens that people can even describe what they look ____4____: tall and slender with huge heads and almond-____5____ eyes. There are models of aliens in the UFO Museum and Research Center in Roswell New Mexico.

_____ 1. (A) digging     (B) lighting     (C) working     (D) covering

_____ 2. (A) In time     (B) In fact     (C) In the long run     (D) In no case

_____ 3. (A) peculiar     (B) rare     (C) strange     (D) common

_____ 4. (A) alike     (B) likely     (C) unlike     (D) like

_____ 5. (A) shaped      (B) shattered      (C) shamed      (D) shouted

**Part C**

The clothes you wear tell something about your personality. They tell the world not only how you want to be seen but how you see yourself ___1___. When someone gives you something to wear that ___2___ your self-image, they're saying, "I agree with you. I like you ___3___ you are." Such a gift should be ___4___ a form of compliment. On the other hand, a gift of clothing that does not match your personality could be a(n) ___5___ to your character. Such gifts between husband and wife can cause ___6___ problems.

Making something by hand has become the ___7___ in many countries today—so much so that giving a homemade gift is considered extraordinary. If you receive a homemade gift, you are lucky. It may not be made ___8___, but it will show a certain quality of love. People who give homemade gifts may be said to be very ___9___. They've given time and emotion, two important characteristics of creativity. No matter what the results of the homemade gift look like, remember it's the thought that ___10___.

_____ 1. (A) either      (B) as well      (C) instead      (D) also

_____ 2. (A) consists of             (B) corresponds to

         (C) complains about        (D) communicates with

_____ 3. (A) what      (B) why      (C) the reason      (D) the way

_____ 4. (A) taken in      (B) taken to      (C) taken as      (D) taken after

_____ 5. (A) insult      (B) flattery      (C) victory      (D) inspiration

_____ 6. (A) marital      (B) medical      (C) mature      (D) marvelous

_____ 7. (A) except      (B) exception      (C) exceptional      (D) exceptionally

_____ 8. (A) perfectly      (B) effectively      (C) timely      (D) patiently

_____ 9. (A) humorous      (B) modest      (C) generous      (D) stingy

_____ 10. (A) trusts      (B) counts      (C) excites      (D) cares

完成日期：_____

實戰語錄

*Opportunity seldom knocks twice.*

機不可失。

# I. Vocabulary

_____ 1. I _____ my ankle when playing basketball. The doctor asked me to rest in bed for a week.

(A) sprained      (B) sprayed      (C) swung      (D) switched

_____ 2. Mr. Wang had gone through all kinds of _____ before he made a name for himself.

(A) hard      (B) harder      (C) hardships      (D) hardly

_____ 3. From the hotel room windows, you can get a _____ view of the distant mountains and the placid lake down below.

(A) thoughtful      (B) enthusiastic      (C) magnificent      (D) disastrous

_____ 4. Children usually feel a lot of _____ on their first day at school.

(A) acquisition      (B) sadness      (C) miracle      (D) anxiety

_____ 5. Everyone in the building _____ when they felt the ground shaking.

(A) screamed      (B) scratched      (C) scattered      (D) scrubbed

_____ 6. Due to the _____, everything costs twice as much as last month.

(A) influence      (B) selfishness      (C) inflation      (D) service

_____ 7. We can only afford to stay in a _____ hotel. The luxurious ones are beyond our means.

(A) modern      (B) moderate      (C) middle      (D) model

_____ 8. Did you hear the noises of wild _____ outside our tent?

(A) pasture      (B) beasts      (C) jungle      (D) streams

_____ 9. The store sells a wide _____ of hats. You can always find the exact hat you want.

(A) construction      (B) decoration      (C) examination      (D) selection

_____ 10. You have to pay heavy customs _____ on the perfume.

(A) fines      (B) penalties      (C) bucks      (D) duties

_____ 11. It is important for a newspaper to make _____ reports of the facts instead of making judgments.

(A) obedient      (B) opposite      (C) objective      (D) offensive

_____ 12. The bee _____ from flower to flower.

(A) escaped      (B) beat      (C) touched      (D) buzzed

_____ 13. She is so _____; she never thinks of others.

    (A) influential     (B) intimate     (C) jealous     (D) selfish

_____ 14. I didn't tell it to her for _____ that she might be upset.

    (A) sake     (B) reason     (C) fear     (D) aim

_____ 15. When you travel to a foreign country, you must bring your _____ with you.

    (A) pet     (B) passport     (C) pest     (D) passenger

_____ 16. Charlie has more _____ than the other lawyers in his firm.

    (A) patients     (B) clients     (C) clerks     (D) customers

_____ 17. I am opposed to hunting because it is against my _____ of respecting all living creatures.

    (A) principals     (B) principles     (C) potentials     (D) periodicals

_____ 18. We watched a caterpillar _____ up the tree.

    (A) dig     (B) sum     (C) stretch     (D) crawl

_____ 19. When we asked Mr. Wang about the current economic situations, he was quite _____ and didn't want to make any comments.

    (A) reserved     (B) open-minded     (C) behaved     (D) determined

_____ 20. Don't carry too much cash with you. You can open a _____ account and then save your money in the bank.

    (A) flourishing     (B) healthy     (C) instinct     (D) deposit

## II. Idioms & Phrases

_____ 1. You would never believe whom I _____ at the airport. I met your sister by chance.

    (A) ran across     (B) ran over     (C) ran out of     (D) ran errands

_____ 2. The child with a serious disease has to be _____ other healthy children in the family.

    (A) prevented from     (B) hidden from

    (C) isolated from     (D) distinguished from

_____ 3. He will _____ desert his children even in face of great danger.

    (A) for certain     (B) by no means     (C) by any means     (D) by the way

_____ 4. Health foods are supposed to be _____ added chemicals.

    (A) particular about     (B) capable of     (C) free of     (D) allergic to

_____ 5. I stopped by the fruit stand to buy some apples _____ home.

    (A) on my way     (B) by the way     (C) in the way     (D) in a way

_____ 6. The soldiers are _____ dangers. They are left unprotected.

    (A) longing for     (B) exposed to     (C) opposed to     (D) insistent on

_____ 7. The government did nothing _____ people's complaints about the terrible traffic.

(A) in return for     (B) in need of     (C) in search of     (D) in response to

_____ 8. Paul was very delighted when his wife _____ a healthy baby.

(A) carried on                 (B) was delivered

(C) kept in her mind    (D) gave birth to

_____ 9. There is always a _____ during rush hour.

(A) keen competition   (B) traffic jam     (C) time machine     (D) time capsule

_____ 10. I _____ a processor. I desire to get one.

(A) grasp at         (B) hang around     (C) itch for         (D) happen upon

# III. Cloze Test

**Part A**

My friend Whit is a professional magician, and he was hired by a restaurant in Los Angeles to ___1___ walk-around, close-up magic each evening. One evening he walked up to a family and began performing. ___2___ a young girl sitting at the table, he asked her to select a card. The girl's father ___3___ him that Wendy, his daughter, was blind.

Whit replied, "That's okay. If it's all right with her, I'd like to try a ___4___ anyway." Then Whit said, "Wendy, would you like to help me with a trick?" Being a little shy, she ___5___ her shoulders and said, "Okay." Whit took a seat ___6___ from her at the table and said, "I'm going to hold up a playing card, Wendy, and it's going to be one of the two colors, ___7___ red or black. What I want you to do is use your psychic powers and tell me what color the card is. You got it?" Wendy nodded. Whit held up the seven of hearts and said, "Is this a red card or a black card?" Wendy said, " Red." Her family smiled. Then Whit held up another card, the three of diamonds and said, "Red or black?" Without ___8___, Wendy said, "Red!" Her family members ___9___ nervously. He went through three more cards, and she got all three right. ___10___, she was five for five! Her father asked Whit whether he was doing some kind of trick or real magic. Whit replied, "You'll have to ask Wendy."

_____ 1. (A) operate       (B) perform       (C) guide         (D) pursue

_____ 2. (A) Changing into   (B) Attacked by    (C) Turning to     (D) Followed by

_____ 3. (A) illustrated     (B) informed      (C) insured       (D) invented

_____ 4. (A) family        (B) sight          (C) note          (D) trick

_____ 5. (A) shook         (B) nodded       (C) stamped      (D) shrugged

_____ 6. (A) cross         (B) crossing      (C) crossed       (D) across

_____ 7. (A) neither       (B) whether      (C) not          (D) either

_____ 8. (A) knowing     (B) hesitating     (C) stopping     (D) replying

_____ 9. (A) giggled     (B) glided     (C) glued     (D) greeted

_____ 10. (A) Incredibly     (B) Honorably     (C) Liberally     (D) Sensitively

## Part B

Where does shyness come from? ____1____ shows that some people are born with a shy temperament. About 20 percent of babies show abnormal signs of distress when they see strangers or encounter ____2____ situations. Some scientists feel that such shyness is ____3____. "Shy parents are more likely to have shy children than outgoing parents," Rita says. "And shyness can be ____4____ determined. We know that Japanese and Taiwanese students are statistically shyer than Israeli students." If 15 to 20 percent of shyness is innate, how do ____5____ people become shy? Children may become shy when they enter school or meet new ____6____. Adolescents may suffer from an identity crisis and become shy. ____7____ can become shy when confronted by problems like divorce or job loss. Here are some ____8____ you can use to help yourself. Don't be perfectionist. You don't have to have the ____9____ joke or the most interesting thing to say before you start a conversation. Don't think the worst. Just open your mouth and say something, and you will find that things work out better than you expected. Learn to take ____10____. Everyone gets refused sometimes in social situations. It is not your fault. It is part of life.

_____ 1. (A) Research     (B) Reflection     (C) Reason     (D) Race

_____ 2. (A) similar     (B) unfamiliar     (C) unforgettable     (D) admiring

_____ 3. (A) industrialized     (B) independent     (C) ignored     (D) inherited

_____ 4. (A) roughly     (B) culturally     (C) favorably     (D) functionally

_____ 5. (A) any     (B) no     (C) other     (D) little

_____ 6. (A) challenges     (B) achievements     (C) fulfillment     (D) chances

_____ 7. (A) Youngsters     (B) Pupils     (C) Professionals     (D) Adults

_____ 8. (A) tips     (B) tops     (C) toes     (D) ties

_____ 9. (A) most boring     (B) funniest     (C) cruelest     (D) most disgusting

_____ 10. (A) welcome     (B) advice     (C) rejection     (D) information

完成日期：_____

實戰語錄

_Experience is the mother of wisdom._
不經一事，不長一智。

# I. Vocabulary

_____ 1. He _____ all his savings from the bank to pay the loan.

    (A) withdrew     (B) deposited     (C) disturbed     (D) contributed

_____ 2. You should _____ your head when there's an emergency.

    (A) hang     (B) lose     (C) keep     (D) strike

_____ 3. It is very important to _____ a balance in the natural world so that all the living creatures can survive.

    (A) maintain     (B) remain     (C) refrain     (D) entertain

_____ 4. Train 205 will delay for 30 minutes—we _____ for any inconvenience caused.

    (A) thank     (B) apologize     (C) worry     (D) confine

_____ 5. Don't be _____. Running away cannot solve the problem.

    (A) ridiculous     (B) efficient     (C) permanent     (D) intensive

_____ 6. He wishes to be a swimming _____, teaching people how to swim.

    (A) advisor     (B) consultant     (C) minister     (D) instructor

_____ 7. You should learn to be _____ about your achievements. There is nothing noble in feeling superior to others.

    (A) confident     (B) modest     (C) careful     (D) persistent

_____ 8. The poor woman had to _____ for food and money for her children.

    (A) beg     (B) earn     (C) save     (D) keep

_____ 9. That is _____ what he said. Actually, I am not very sure.

    (A) luckily     (B) miserably     (C) exactly     (D) roughly

_____ 10. The coat is of very _____ material. It will last several years.

    (A) warm     (B) durable     (C) waterproof     (D) heat-resistant

_____ 11. With the recession in economy, it seems impossible for our company to achieve the _____ of a 10% increase in sales.

    (A) explosive     (B) objective     (C) relative     (D) competitive

_____ 12. They displayed their valuable pieces of china in a glass-fronted _____.

    (A) cabin     (B) cabinet     (C) cable     (D) cafeteria

_____ 13. The company sends customers free _____ of shampoo.

    (A) lectures     (B) medals     (C) napkins     (D) samples

_____ 14. Every _____ of her face is attractive.

    (A) feature     (B) detail     (C) account     (D) illustration

_____ 15. You must have a _____ to get access to these classified files.

(A) passport  (B) passion  (C) passage  (D) password

_____ 16. It costs a lot of money to feed and _____ five children.

(A) cloth  (B) clothe  (C) clothes  (D) clothing

_____ 17. In court, everyone should have equal rights; no one can enjoy any _____.

(A) advantages  (B) benefits  (C) privileges  (D) profits

_____ 18. All the passengers died in the crash, including the pilot and the _____.

(A) crew  (B) crow  (C) claw  (D) crowd

_____ 19. In the will, the old man left the house and his business to his wife and son _____.

(A) respectively  (B) respectably  (C) respectfully  (D) individually

_____ 20. Could you _____ how the robber looked like in detail?

(A) prescribe  (B) inscribe  (C) describe  (D) ascribe

## II. Idioms & Phrases

_____ 1. The boy unwillingly turned off the TV set and went back to his room _____.

(A) under the weather  (B) under protest  (C) on the condition  (D) with gratitude

_____ 2. You can always _____ me when you are in need.

(A) stand for  (B) cope with  (C) count on  (D) bless for

_____ 3. Rome is a city which _____ visiting.

(A) is worthy  (B) famous for  (C) is worth  (D) does without

_____ 4. He _____ pressures from work and family, and in the end committed suicide.

(A) was convinced of  (B) was driven to extremes by  (C) was relieved of  (D) was called upon by

_____ 5. People with hearing problems can communicate _____ sign language.

(A) by means of  (B) in regard to  (C) for lack of  (D) with a view to

_____ 6. Careless campers were _____ starting the forest fire.

(A) blamed for  (B) praised for  (C) curious about  (D) longing for

_____ 7. Don't reject me _____ God.

(A) as much as  (B) instead of  (C) for the sake of  (D) by the way of

_____ 8. Are you _____ for work?

(A) geared up  (B) looked up  (C) mixed up  (D) drawn up

_____ 9. He was _____ nervous even though it was the first time he stood on the stage and faced such a large audience.

(A) nothing but  (B) next to  (C) all but  (D) not in the least

_____ 10. _____ the interview, it was gradually clear that she was not suitable for the job.

    (A) With a view to    (B) In the course of    (C) As for    (D) With respect to

## III. Cloze Test

**( Part A )**

    Without stopping to think, Mei Ling struggled and climbed through the half-open window of the car and ____1____ her little body inside. She unbuckled the ____2____ that held the ____3____ child and then tried to free the man in front. Since the doors were tightly ____4____, there was only one way to get him out of the car—through the window. Mei Ling lost no time. She helped the man push himself through the window, which she herself opened wider. It took a great ____5____ of effort to push the man, who was several ____6____ her size, before he managed to get through. Mei Ling then turned to the frightened child, picked him up in her arms and ____7____ him to his father. However, she now found herself in a precarious ____8____. She had become too tired to climb out of the window of the car. By this time, the crowd had become ____9____ what was going on in the car, and many people started milling around, though they hung back seeing the hood of the car beginning to ____10____ smoke.

_____ 1. (A) squeezed    (B) swelled    (C) surrounded    (D) strengthened

_____ 2. (A) thread    (B) tunnel    (C) belt    (D) sink

_____ 3. (A) delighted    (B) embarrassed    (C) discouraged    (D) frightened

_____ 4. (A) jammed    (B) achieved    (C) limited    (D) focused

_____ 5. (A) deal    (B) number    (C) sum    (D) plenty

_____ 6. (A) averages    (B) numbers    (C) volumes    (D) times

_____ 7. (A) advanced    (B) circled    (C) handed    (D) dressed

_____ 8. (A) suggestion    (B) situation    (C) sentence    (D) sensitivity

_____ 9. (A) aware    (B) unsure    (C) disposed    (D) accused

_____ 10. (A) give up    (B) hold up    (C) hold on    (D) give out

**( Part B )**

    Papa Joe was a quiet little old man of eighty, but he was energetic ____1____ his age. Having no family that he could call his own, and having nowhere to go, like many old people, he ____2____ the library, especially in the afternoons, only to enjoy a fleeting ____3____ with books, newspapers and magazines. Mr. Simpson, the librarian, could not send him away because Papa Joe caused no trouble.

    One afternoon, Papa Joe had one of his usual ____4____ of dizziness and would have collapsed ____5____ the prompt attention of Mr. Simpson, who helped the old man ____6____ his

feet. The librarian gently escorted the old man to a comfortable chair, ___7___ up his things that had fallen in disarray on the library floor, and finally took him to the staff room where he offered him some hot tea. A few weeks after the ___8___, Papa Joe came to Mr. Simpson and said, "you're very kind, Mr. Simpson. You're the only real friend I have in my old age. You may not believe me, but I have a lot of money in my safekeeping. I promise I will leave it all to you in my ___9___." Astonished at this ___10___ reaction to his kindness, Mr. Simpson could only utter "Me?" He then turned away, leaving the confused but excited Mr. Simpson alone.

_____ 1. (A) in spite of     (B) in case of     (C) in that     (D) in regard to

_____ 2. (A) frequented     (B) frustrated     (C) furnished     (D) fueled

_____ 3. (A) admission     (B) accuracy     (C) acquaintance     (D) adjustment

_____ 4. (A) wells     (B) tales     (C) spells     (D) bills

_____ 5. (A) but for     (B) only for     (C) as for     (D) for all

_____ 6. (A) by     (B) to     (C) with     (D) through

_____ 7. (A) tidied     (B) messed     (C) tore     (D) erased

_____ 8. (A) conflict     (B) encounter     (C) incident     (D) tragedy

_____ 9. (A) negotiation     (B) claim     (C) will     (D) contract

_____ 10. (A) expected     (B) unexpected     (C) unexpectedly     (D) expectant

完成日期：_____

實戰語錄

*Slow and sure wins the race.*
慢而穩者得勝。

## I. Vocabulary

_____ 1. She pulled me by the _____ of my shirt and told me she wanted to go to the bathroom.

(A) scarf      (B) sleeve      (C) socks      (D) cap

_____ 2. Never forget to wear a _____ to protect your head when riding on a motorcycle.

(A) handle      (B) harvest      (C) helmet      (D) harmonica

_____ 3. A large _____ of the population is in favor of the recent reforms in the educational system.

(A) amount      (B) number      (C) majority      (D) sum

_____ 4. The idea of sleeping in on Sunday is quite _____ to me.

(A) appealing      (B) appetizing      (C) strong      (D) confused

_____ 5. Although the food is expensive, I enjoy the good _____ at the restaurant.

(A) interference      (B) observation      (C) service      (D) limitation

_____ 6. Many scholars and _____ gathered in the coffee shop, talking about the presidential election.

(A) intellectuals      (B) physicians      (C) managers      (D) grocers

_____ 7. The students are practicing the conversation with each other, while the teacher is _____ the whole activity.

(A) monitoring      (B) suspecting      (C) judging      (D) teaching

_____ 8. The kid always _____ badly when guests come to visit.

(A) creates      (B) behaves      (C) decorates      (D) fascinates

_____ 9. He has no _____ of humor. He was angry when I played a trick on him.

(A) glory      (B) direction      (C) sense      (D) favor

_____ 10. Are you in real _____ in saying so?

(A) heart      (B) intention      (C) earnest      (D) tendency

_____ 11. It is the job of an astronomer to _____ the stars in space.

(A) overlook      (B) observe      (C) follow      (D) calculate

_____ 12. Please put more _____ on the spaghetti. It will be more delicious.

(A) mustache      (B) sauce      (C) leather      (D) grace

_____ 13. Disease is the _____ of mankind.

(A) enemy      (B) publisher      (C) lecturer      (D) fellow

_____ 14. The teacher is _____ enough to explain the lesson over and over again until

every student understands.

    (A) accurate        (B) remote       (C) intelligent     (D) patient

_____ 15. He marked his girlfriend's birthday on the _____.

    (A) customs       (B) opera        (C) calendar       (D) history

_____ 16. The first mobile phones were _____ to carry but now they are much lighter.

    (A) clumsy        (B) easy        (C) suitable       (D) inappropriate

_____ 17. You must follow the proper _____ for applying for a visa.

    (A) promotion      (B) progress      (C) procedure     (D) provision

_____ 18. How can I have any self-confidence when you are always _____ of me?

    (A) proud        (B) cruel        (C) ambitious      (D) critical

_____ 19. The clip from the old newspaper _____ me of the terrible accident that happened in my youth.

    (A) recalled      (B) remembered    (C) reminded     (D) reflected

_____ 20. She does such a good job that she _____ every penny she earns.

    (A) demands      (B) deserves      (C) desires      (D) deserts

## II. Idioms & Phrases

_____ 1. These peaches must be very expensive for they are _____.

    (A) out of season   (B) once upon a time  (C) all of a sudden   (D) by heart

_____ 2. My neighbors always _____ my house when I am away on vacation.

    (A) see eye to eye with         (B) make eyes at

    (C) have an eye for           (D) keep an eye on

_____ 3. They built a monument _____ the people who died during the earthquake.

    (A) in place of     (B) in memory of    (C) in company with  (D) in favor of

_____ 4. All the roads out of the village were _____ by the police.

    (A) blocked out    (B) blocked in     (C) blocked off    (D) blocked up

_____ 5. We took a map with us just to be _____.

    (A) on the safe side  (B) little by little   (C) on average     (D) once and for all

_____ 6. Don't be afraid. _____ your courage and fight against your opponent.

    (A) Speed up     (B) Pull up      (C) Gather up     (D) Cheer up

_____ 7. The boy broke his toy _____ to attract the attention of his parents.

    (A) by mistake           (B) for the convenience

    (C) on purpose           (D) face to face

_____ 8. There is no need to _____ for your brother. Obviously, he is guilty.

    (A) tear up       (B) dry up       (C) warm up      (D) cover up

_____ 9. The program took so much time that it was completed several weeks _____.

     (A) in time      (B) once in a while    (C) all of a sudden    (D) behind schedule

_____ 10. You must study harder since you have _____ the other students.

     (A) fallen over      (B) fallen behind     (C) fallen beneath    (D) fallen under

## III. Cloze Test

### Part A

Many kinds of music can stir the imagination and produce strong feelings. Romantic composers such as Chopin and Tchaikovsky enhance feelings of love and ___1___. Religious and spiritual music can help some people feel peaceful or ___2___ their pain. But one musician seems to have a(n) ___3___ ability to heal the human body—Wolfgang Amadeus Mozart. Scientists have found his music to be ___4___ in its ability to calm its listeners. It can also increase their perceptions, and help them ___5___ themselves more clearly.

Many amazing cases have been documented using Mozart as a ___6___ aid. For example, a ___7___ premature baby named Krissy, who ___8___ only 1.5 pounds at birth, was on total life support. Doctors thought she had little chance of ___9___. Her mother insisted on playing Mozart for Krissy. She believed it could ___10___ her daughter's life. Krissy lived, but she was very small for her age and slower than the average child.

_____ 1. (A) compassion     (B) cruelty     (C) collection     (D) curiosity

_____ 2. (A) increase     (B) advance     (C) multiply     (D) lessen

_____ 3. (A) common     (B) unique     (C) average     (D) frequent

_____ 4. (A) terrible     (B) sympathetic     (C) ordinary     (D) remarkable

_____ 5. (A) express     (B) shrink     (C) withdraw     (D) affect

_____ 6. (A) humming     (B) harming     (C) healing     (D) hearing

_____ 7. (A) enormous     (B) vast     (C) tiny     (D) huge

_____ 8. (A) weight     (B) weighed     (C) wore     (D) wasted

_____ 9. (A) surroundings     (B) surface     (C) survival     (D) survey

_____ 10. (A) save     (B) ruin     (C) reject     (D) cherish

### Part B

The Taipei Tree Frog has a green back and is yellow underneath. When ___1___, they can change color so their natural enemies can't see them. They can climb trees to ___2___ prey. The reason they can do this is because they have discs on ___3___ of their toes. These enable them to cling to vertical surfaces. The Taipei Tree Frog is the only frog ___4___ in Taiwan that builds its own nest. The male frog uses its hind legs and body to dig holes ___5___ the banks

of still water. The female frog ____6____ 300 to 400 eggs in a white foamy mess like ____7____, hidden in roots of grasses or under rocks. As our cities ____8____, we are taking away the Taipei Tree Frog's habitat. They are now a ____9____ species. There are still many of them in the wild, ____10____ we don't make plans for them, one day we may never see them again.

_____ 1. (A) in safety    (B) in danger    (C) in itself    (D) in poverty

_____ 2. (A) hunt for    (B) play with    (C) eat up    (D) keep up with

_____ 3. (A) the backs    (B) the fronts    (C) the tips    (D) the bottoms

_____ 4. (A) species    (B) beasts    (C) monsters    (D) mammals

_____ 5. (A) with    (B) in    (C) out    (D) along

_____ 6. (A) hatches    (B) deposits    (C) boils    (D) breaks

_____ 7. (A) bulbs    (B) bugs    (C) bullets    (D) bubbles

_____ 8. (A) expand    (B) explore    (C) explode    (D) exhaust

_____ 9. (A) dangerous    (B) memorable    (C) protected    (D) talkative

_____ 10. (A) but if    (B) only until    (C) even though    (D) for fear that

完成日期：_____

實戰語錄

*Patience is a virtue.*
小不忍則亂大謀。

## I. Vocabulary

_____ 1. Computer is a(n) _____ invention. It has changed the way people live.

     (A) conservative     (B) exceptional     (C) revolutionary     (D) flexible

_____ 2. A(n) _____ was sent out to rescue two injured people in the deep mountain.

     (A) heater     (B) gangster     (C) helicopter     (D) instructor

_____ 3. Good _____ of time is very important to people who work on a tight schedule.

     (A) judgment     (B) management     (C) advertisement     (D) supplement

_____ 4. I'd like to make a(n) _____ with Dr. Miller this evening, please.

     (A) date     (B) influence     (C) operation     (D) appointment

_____ 5. His joke was so funny that we _____ with laughter.

     (A) roared     (B) murmured     (C) panicked     (D) adapted

_____ 6. I took an _____ course in English last summer.

     (A) intense     (B) intensive     (C) intensified     (D) intensely

_____ 7. With proper inducement, curiosity can be turned into a strong _____ for learning.

     (A) objection     (B) quotation     (C) suspicion     (D) motivation

_____ 8. She _____ to a tennis club which is very hard to get into.

     (A) confines     (B) lends     (C) belongs     (D) relates

_____ 9. He broke the _____ of daily life. He went to see a play instead of going to school.

     (A) gravity     (B) silence     (C) routine     (D) chorus

_____ 10. The medicine did _____ my pain in five minutes.

     (A) emerge     (B) effect     (C) erase     (D) ease

_____ 11. You should not run away from the _____ but face them and try to overcome them.

     (A) spectacles     (B) obstacles     (C) articles     (D) periodicals

_____ 12. The endless shaking hands is an inevitable part of an election _____.

     (A) motion     (B) campaign     (C) competition     (D) candidate

_____ 13. Stand on the _____ and you can know how much you weigh.

     (A) gown     (B) fountain     (C) crayon     (D) scale

_____ 14. He is a _____ writer. He has written 139 books.

     (A) productive     (B) numerous     (C) new     (D) cultivated

_____ 15. He is a _____ citizen who is always ready to defend his country.

    (A) passive      (B) patriotic      (C) stubborn      (D) considerate

_____ 16. The road was so _____ that it was dangerous to walk on it.

    (A) smooth      (B) slippery      (C) mild      (D) coarse

_____ 17. We apologize for any inconvenience caused in the _____ of refurnishing our hotel rooms.

    (A) process      (B) procession      (C) procedure      (D) pursuit

_____ 18. The main _____ grown here for export are coffee and cotton.

    (A) harvests      (B) goods      (C) crops      (D) products

_____ 19. The Queen wore her _____ and robes to attend the ceremony.

    (A) pajamas      (B) slippers      (C) crown      (D) stick

_____ 20. The doctors made one last _____ attempt to save the girl's life.

    (A) fundamental      (B) prevailing      (C) profitable      (D) desperate

## II. Idioms & Phrases

_____ 1. The rock band is popular with young people, and girls, _____, are attracted to the handsome singers.

    (A) in return      (B) in particular      (C) in case      (D) in private

_____ 2. My kite was _____ so I had to run after it.

    (A) blown out      (B) blown up      (C) blown over      (D) blown away

_____ 3. She _____ my idea by saying that it won't work at all.

    (A) gave a ring to               (B) draw the line at

    (C) asked a favor of           (D) poured cold water on

_____ 4. People _____ him because he wore very strange boots.

    (A) made fun of      (B) went too far into    (C) gained over      (D) gambled on

_____ 5. Call me _____ you arrive.

    (A) as fast as      (B) as soon as      (C) as far as      (D) as well as

_____ 6. I think I'll _____ if I don't take a vacation soon.

    (A) go crazy      (B) back up      (C) cheer up      (D) calm down

_____ 7. The bank cashier managed to steal money from the customer's account _____.

    (A) behind the scenes   (B) by heart      (C) on the spot      (D) in a new light

_____ 8. To everyone's disappointment, the government's new policy _____.

    (A) fell flat      (B) ran out      (C) fell sick      (D) fell short

_____ 9. Nobody dared to talk loudly _____ the principal.

    (A) in the front of   (B) in the order of    (C) in the presence of (D) at the price of

_____ 10. I can't believe the theater has been fully _____ .

    (A) booked up     (B) stared at     (C) driven away     (D) laid off

## III. Cloze Test

### Part A

School observation is a practical and direct approach to evaluate a school. Maybe it is easy to know a school from many ____1____ of information, such as media reports, government ____2____ and school publications. However, it is ____3____ to judge a school. There is a ____4____ between reports and truths because possibly some bias and blind spots ____5____ in the information. In other words, a school highly ____6____ by parents and the society may not be satisfactory. ____7____, spending a period of time making observations or ____8____ will be one of the best ways to understand how a school is ____9____. The process of observation can also be ____10____ for school improvement.

_____ 1. (A) aspects     (B) classes     (C) walks     (D) levels

_____ 2. (A) controls     (B) documents     (C) offices     (D) rules

_____ 3. (A) fair     (B) easy     (C) interesting     (D) difficult

_____ 4. (A) secret     (B) distinction     (C) rumor     (D) policy

_____ 5. (A) reveal     (B) isolate     (C) exist     (D) imply

_____ 6. (A) criticized     (B) questioned     (C) valued     (D) shared

_____ 7. (A) Instead     (B) On the contrary     (C) In the same way     (D) As a result

_____ 8. (A) comments     (B) advantages     (C) inspection     (D) repairs

_____ 9. (A) running     (B) located     (C) constructed     (D) teaching

_____ 10. (A) assigned     (B) provided     (C) attracted     (D) added

### Part B

Most problems with memory are the result of bad habits. If you allow yourself to____1____ the habit of not paying attention to the world and not making an effort to remember things, your memory will begin to decrease. A good memory ____2____ is the result of good habits. There is nothing magical or mysterious about it. If you want to lose weight, you must change your eating ____3____. Similarly, if you want to improve your memory, you should change ____4____ you deal with information. Here are some tips to help you improve your memory. If you practice these techniques over a period of time, you should notice a great improvement in your ability to ____5____ things.

Set realistic goals. Don't expect to be able to remember everything. At first, you can ____6____ things which you are familiar with. And then try to work on areas where you

_____7_____ the greatest memory problems in the past.

Stay mentally _____8_____. When you exercise your mind, it stays sharp. If you avoid mental challenges, your memory will begin to lose its ability to handle those challenging problems.

_____9_____ activities that do not encourage you to think. Many TV programs require no mental input at all. You don't have to think while you are watching a program purely for entertainment. You can easily _____10_____ the habit of turning off your brain when you watch TV.

_____ 1. (A) break into    (B) slip into    (C) look into    (D) run across

_____ 2. (A) in other words    (B) on the other hand    (C) most importantly    (D) moreover

_____ 3. (A) customs    (B) actions    (C) habits    (D) behavior

_____ 4. (A) the reason    (B) the way    (C) the time    (D) the place

_____ 5. (A) remember    (B) call    (C) remind    (D) remove

_____ 6. (A) carry on    (B) live on    (C) focus on    (D) depend on

_____ 7. (A) encountered    (B) encouraged    (C) depressed    (D) humiliated

_____ 8. (A) massive    (B) negative    (C) passive    (D) active

_____ 9. (A) Look up to    (B) Take part in    (C) Put up with    (D) Cut down on

_____ 10. (A) pick on    (B) pick off    (C) pick up    (D) pick out

完成日期：_____

實戰語錄

*It is the unexpected that always happens.*
天有不測風雲，人有旦夕禍福。

## I. Vocabulary

_____ 1. I have a very tight _____ this week. I am afraid that I cannot go shopping with you.

    (A) screwdriver    (B) shepherd    (C) sentence    (D) schedule

_____ 2. Every part of the building is _____ with the whole.

    (A) harmful    (B) harmonious    (C) harsh    (D) hard

_____ 3. Table _____ vary in different cultures, so it is advisable to follow the examples of native people.

    (A) manners    (B) politeness    (C) methods    (D) senses

_____ 4. I see it's _____ lunchtime, so let's go get something to eat.

    (A) against    (B) approaching    (C) passing    (D) spending

_____ 5. Taiwan is _____ from Mainland China by the Taiwan Strait.

    (A) approached    (B) calculated    (C) declared    (D) separated

_____ 6. Don't _____ in my affairs.

    (A) interest    (B) insult    (C) inspect    (D) interfere

_____ 7. _____ choice questions are easier than blank-filling because you don't have to come up with the answers yourself. All you have to do is choose from the answers provided.

    (A) Additional    (B) Descriptive    (C) Numerous    (D) Multiple

_____ 8. I feel that I have _____ greatly from his wits.

    (A) damaged    (B) educated    (C) emphasized    (D) benefited

_____ 9. Mr. Black felt great _____ over the success of his project.

    (A) infection    (B) satisfaction    (C) motivation    (D) election

_____ 10. The government exercises _____ control over what is shown in the newspaper.

    (A) editorial    (B) military    (C) energy    (D) system

_____ 11. Normally, a person must pass a test to _____ the citizenship of the U.S.

    (A) retain    (B) obtain    (C) sustain    (D) contain

_____ 12. There is a really impressive art center on the _____ at my university.

    (A) campus    (B) professor    (C) course    (D) department

_____ 13. He promised to _____ the problem. He wanted to make a satisfactory arrangement.

    (A) contribute    (B) settle    (C) exaggerate    (D) isolate

_____ 14. Many people are interested in science _____.

(A) fiction      (B) essay      (C) romance      (D) album

_____ 15. I had a _____ afternoon all by myself, drinking tea and listening to soft music.

(A) shocking      (B) frightening      (C) chilly      (D) peaceful

_____ 16. I need a _____ to make a phone call.

(A) bill      (B) check      (C) coin      (D) dial

_____ 17. The manufacturers must guarantee the quality of their _____.

(A) production      (B) produce      (C) productivity      (D) products

_____ 18. He is crippled and he can't walk without a _____.

(A) cub      (B) crutch      (C) cone      (D) craft

_____ 19. Severe _____ are placed on the sale of alcohol.

(A) descriptions      (B) destructions      (C) restrictions      (D) instructions

_____ 20. _____ the fact that there was almost no hope of finding the missing man, the search still went on.

(A) Despite      (B) Identity      (C) Unless      (D) Opposed

## II. Idioms & Phrases

_____ 1. _____, my best friend came to my birthday party without informing me.

(A) For example          (B) To my surprise

(C) Generally speaking          (D) From time to time

_____ 2. He spoke _____ the protesters. He supported them.

(A) in combination with          (B) in company with

(C) in possession of          (D) in favor of

_____ 3. He repeated the same story _____.

(A) off and on      (B) over and over      (C) up and down      (D) inside and out

_____ 4. Since they don't have enough money in hand, they decide to pay the car _____.

(A) on credit          (B) in cash

(C) before long          (D) as soon as possible

_____ 5. There _____ treasures buried in the cave by the pirates.

(A) used to have      (B) used to be      (C) has been said      (D) has had

_____ 6. The test was _____ easy. I could only answer half of the questions.

(A) nothing but      (B) kind of      (C) far from      (D) by far

_____ 7. I cannot make arrangements for a big dinner party _____.

(A) at such short notice          (B) one by one

(C) to the point          (D) as a result

_____ 8. Extra information will be found _____ the page.

(A) belonging to  (B) according to  (C) at the bottom of  (D) crowded with

_____ 9. It _____ that you get nothing without hard work.

(A) is up to you  (B) makes no sense

(C) jumps to conclusions  (D) goes without saying

_____ 10. The wound proved _____ him. He died of it.

(A) fatal to  (B) loyal to  (C) attached to  (D) committed to

## III. Cloze Test

### Part A

All over the world, there are millions of people who ___1___ or never eat meat. These people are ___2___ vegetarians. To people ___3___ eat meat, being a vegetarian may seem like a very ___4___ way to live, but most vegetarians are very happy with their choice of diet. They choose their diets for several ___5___ reasons.

Some vegetarians eat almost anything ___6___ food that actually comes from the killing of live animals. Their diets may or may not include fish and other seafood, but usually include milk and other ___7___ products and eggs. Some vegetarians are only ___8___ vegetarians. They eat meat products occasionally, on social and special ___9___, but they generally try to avoid doing so. ___10___, there are some extreme vegetarians who avoid eating anything that comes from animals, including milk, cheese and eggs.

_____ 1. (A) often  (B) rarely  (C) frequently  (D) always

_____ 2. (A) elected  (B) called  (C) ordered  (D) suspected

_____ 3. (A) what  (B) which  (C) who  (D) those

_____ 4. (A) strange  (B) excellent  (C) acceptable  (D) ordinary

_____ 5. (A) similar  (B) dependent  (C) informative  (D) different

_____ 6. (A) except  (B) besides  (C) but for  (D) as well as

_____ 7. (A) seafood  (B) poultry  (C) dairy  (D) flesh

_____ 8. (A) rarely  (B) scarcely  (C) reluctant  (D) sometimes

_____ 9. (A) atmosphere  (B) calculation  (C) dormitories  (D) occasions

_____ 10. (A) On the other hand  (B) In other words

(C) As a result  (D) As a matter of fact

### Part B

Mark: John, I hear that you're looking for an apartment to rent. Have you had any ___1___ finding one?

John: No, I've been ___2___ for the past three weeks trying to find a place, but everything is

too expensive.

Mark: Have you looked at the _____3_____ listings in the newspaper?

John: Yeah, I used them to look at _____4_____ apartments, but I didn't find anything in my price range.

Mark: Why do you want to move into your own place anyway?

John: Living at home has been _____5_____ gloom and doom. My parents are so _____6_____ and I have practically no freedom to do what I want.

Mark: Why don't you move in with me? I have a little two-bedroom _____7_____ and wouldn't mind having a roommate.

John: That's a fabulous idea! _____8_____ how extraordinary it would be if you and I lived together.

Mark: Yeah, living together would also _____9_____ the rent. My only request, however, is that you keep the apartment neat. I'm really _____10_____ a dirty place.

John: No problem. Thanks a lot, Mark, I knew I could count on you.

_____ 1. (A) luck     (B) misfortune     (C) evil     (D) favor

_____ 2. (A) on the road     (B) in the way     (C) off the road     (D) by the way

_____ 3. (A) fatal     (B) mental     (C) gentle     (D) rental

_____ 4. (A) a large amount of     (B) a variety of     (C) a great deal of     (D) a slice of

_____ 5. (A) nothing like     (B) nothing of     (C) nothing but     (D) nothing about

_____ 6. (A) annoyed     (B) annoying     (C) pleasing     (D) pleased

_____ 7. (A) house     (B) mansion     (C) hostel     (D) apartment

_____ 8. (A) See     (B) Judge     (C) Know     (D) Imagine

_____ 9. (A) raise     (B) reduce     (C) declare     (D) cease

_____ 10. (A) fond of     (B) picky about     (C) proud of     (D) jealous of

完成日期：_____

實戰語錄

*After a storm comes a calm.*

雨過天青。

## I. Vocabulary

_____ 1. You should take my words _____. I say it for your own good.

(A) seriously      (B) easy      (C) lightly      (D) legally

_____ 2. Our team will play volleyball at the _____.

(A) jail      (B) gallery      (C) gymnasium      (D) court

_____ 3. People who do _____ jobs usually have to work harder but get lower pay.

(A) mental      (B) dangerous      (C) manual      (D) elaborate

_____ 4. Most people think the _____ should take the responsibility for the collapse of the building.

(A) adventurer      (B) advertiser      (C) architect      (D) actor

_____ 5. He took the _____ of losing his life to save the drowning boy.

(A) defense      (B) election      (C) exposure      (D) risk

_____ 6. Industrial robots are more _____ than human workers.

(A) effective      (B) original      (C) sensible      (D) efficient

_____ 7. He tried to hide his nervousness, but instead made it even more _____.

(A) envious      (B) obvious      (C) previous      (D) gracious

_____ 8. Tomorrow's football match is _____ owing to the bad weather.

(A) started      (B) canceled      (C) disappeared      (D) forbidden

_____ 9. You _____ me by standing at the window all in white.

(A) invited      (B) organized      (C) prepared      (D) scared

_____ 10. It was so dark that I couldn't make out the _____ in the dark.

(A) field      (B) fight      (C) fence      (D) figure

_____ 11. He has a _____ habit of sleeping with his glasses on.

(A) particular      (B) individual      (C) unique      (D) peculiar

_____ 12. Thousands of buildings _____ in the serious earthquake.

(A) collapsed      (B) burned      (C) erected      (D) invaded

_____ 13. _____ has it that war will break out. Many people have left the country.

(A) Rule      (B) Rush      (C) Rumor      (D) Rust

_____ 14. He _____ all his energy in helping disabled people.

(A) saved      (B) invested      (C) took      (D) cost

_____ 15. Nowadays, quite a few young people want to enter the legal _____. They believe being a lawyer is a profitable job.

       (A) lawsuit        (B) procession      (C) profession      (D) possession

_____ 16. The _____ between the East and the West are greatly different.

       (A) cultures        (B) cues          (C) curls          (D) cushions

_____ 17. The old woman is _____ something which I have difficulty hearing clearly.

       (A) murmuring      (B) remarking      (C) discussing      (D) arguing

_____ 18. _____ finally tracked down the killer, who had murdered over 20 people.

       (A) Mayors        (B) Detectives      (C) Bankers       (D) Journalists

_____ 19. The young man felt offended when his invitation was _____ by the girl.

       (A) rejected       (B) rebelled      (C) disagreed      (D) disapproved

_____ 20. I believe I will get there earlier than you. Let's _____ on that.

       (A) bet         (B) rely         (C) depend       (D) count

## II. Idioms & Phrases

_____ 1. The bus is so crowded that it is _____ impossible to make room for one more person.

       (A) anything but    (B) for lack of      (C) next to       (D) no more than

_____ 2. Don't listen to him. He is as _____ and is very likely to cheat you.

       (A) cool as a cucumber           (B) fierce as a lion

       (C) cunning as a fox            (D) timid as a rabbit

_____ 3. Most of us _____ our parents' love _____ and do not value it.

       (A) put...into practice         (B) carry...around

       (C) push...aside             (D) take...for granted

_____ 4. The car _____ on our way to school; thus we were all late today.

       (A) broke out      (B) broke in       (C) broke off      (D) broke down

_____ 5. The old man felt _____ when he was sitting with a large crowd of young people at the rock concert.

       (A) at large       (B) out of place    (C) in line        (D) in a mess

_____ 6. After a year, she was _____ the cancer.

       (A) charged with    (B) cured of      (C) converted into    (D) interfered with

_____ 7. You must not run away. You have to _____.

       (A) face the music    (B) lose face      (C) make faces     (D) face to face

_____ 8. He _____ his company's expansion by setting up chain stores.

       (A) brought up     (B) brought out    (C) brought down    (D) brought about

_____ 9. Throughout the race, Steve was _____, and no one was able to catch up with him.

(A) looking forward    (B) taking the lead    (C) making his point    (D) in motion

_____ 10. The director's new film _____ the relationship between a woman and her unfaithful husband.

(A) helps out              (B) pops up              (C) turns out              (D) deals with

## III. Cloze Test

( Part A )

Telephones, television sets, radios and computers—all of these are communication __1__. Because of these machines, people can spread ideas and news quickly all over the world. For example, __2__, people in many parts of the world can know the results of an election in Canada, Japan or Australia. An international soccer match comes into the homes of sports lovers __3__—on their television sets. News of a natural disaster __4__ an earthquake or a flood can bring help from distant countries within hours. Even __5__, a businessperson can participate in a business meeting. A worldwide network of communication system makes all these possible.

By the system of e-mail, the message has traveled much faster than any ordinary letter. The whole message has traveled faster than an ordinary telephone message too. One reason is the new kind of telephone line. These telephone lines are __6__: they are glass. The __7__ using glass is called "fiber optics." These long stands of glass can carry many messages __8__. They also receive signals from __9__ high above the Earth. The satellites __10__, or receive and send again, from one part of the world to another. These messages travel down the information highway in an instant, at a speed near the speed of light.

_____ 1. (A) devices           (B) details            (C) desire            (D) defeats
_____ 2. (A) for good          (B) once in a while    (C) little by little  (D) in seconds
_____ 3. (A) whereby           (B) everywhere         (C) nowhere           (D) somewhere
_____ 4. (A) in spite of       (B) in addition        (C) such as           (D) in the long run
_____ 5. (A) on fire           (B) on vacation        (C) on the job        (D) on a diet
_____ 6. (A) common            (B) special            (C) ordinary          (D) difficult
_____ 7. (A) technology        (B) trick              (C) tendency          (D) territory
_____ 8. (A) for the past few years            (B) for a very long while
            (C) on and off                         (D) at the same time
_____ 9. (A) suburbs           (B) strategies         (C) shepherds         (D) satellites
_____ 10. (A) transmit          (B) threaten           (C) translate         (D) trap

( Part B )

Michelle:  Today, I heard some really __1__ news about our friend Tom.

Ricky: I would consider Tom ____2____ a fool than my friend. That guy is always getting himself in trouble. ____3____ has he done now?

Michelle: I heard that he ____4____ to the casino almost every night and gambles his money away.

Ricky: Does he think that gambling is a career path or that he can ____5____ at the casino?

Michelle: I don't know. All I know is that his wife Mary is all worked ____6____ over the situation.

Ricky: What is she saying about Tom's gambling problem?

Michelle: She says that ____7____ to get along with and that he often erupts in ____8____.

Ricky: That's terrible. What should we do?

Michelle: I've observed in the past in cases such as these that it is wrong to place blame. We cannot ____9____ force Tom to quit gambling for good, but we can ____10____ him to seek counseling for his problem.

Ricky: That's just what we can do now.

_____ 1. (A) disturb      (B) disturbed      (C) disturbing      (D) disturbance

_____ 2. (A) much of      (B) more of      (C) less of      (D) some of

_____ 3. (A) Where      (B) How      (C) Why      (D) What

_____ 4. (A) gets his way      (B) has his way      (C) demands his way      (D) make his way

_____ 5. (A) make a judgment            (B) make a living

       (C) make an error            (D) make both ends meet

_____ 6. (A) down      (B) up      (C) off      (D) at

_____ 7. (A) it is easy      (B) he feels at ease      (C) he is not easy      (D) it is not easy

_____ 8. (A) peace      (B) violence      (C) curiosity      (D) poverty

_____ 9. (A) purposely      (B) psychologically      (C) hardly      (D) physically

_____ 10. (A) discourage      (B) impress      (C) insure      (D) encourage

完成日期：_____

實戰語錄

*Never make two bites of a cherry.*

一氣呵成。

# I. Vocabulary

_____ 1. In the first stanza, "heard" _____ with "bird."

    (A) shares        (B) associates        (C) connects        (D) rhymes

_____ 2. The _____ of the big computer company are in Taipei.

    (A) stations        (B) downtowns        (C) shelters        (D) headquarters

_____ 3. When I read a book, I usually write my comments in the _____ of the pages.

    (A) whites        (B) emptiness        (C) holes        (D) margins

_____ 4. The writer's latest book has so far _____ little interest.

    (A) arisen        (B) risen        (C) aroused        (D) raised

_____ 5. The police _____ the whole area for the missing boy.

    (A) greeted        (B) searched        (C) horrified        (D) indicated

_____ 6. I tell my _____ friend about everything that troubles me.

    (A) mutual        (B) intimate        (C) fresh        (D) false

_____ 7. As the number of cars has _____, the traffic has become more crowded.

    (A) mushroomed        (B) declined        (C) decreased        (D) divided

_____ 8. I've got nothing to tell you _____ what I have already said.

    (A) beyond        (B) beneath        (C) below        (D) behind

_____ 9. Yamingshan is famous for its beautiful _____. Many tourists go there every year.

    (A) scenery        (B) capacity        (C) volume        (D) definition

_____ 10. To make your ideas clear, you must _____ unnecessary arguments from the essay.

    (A) clean        (B) empty        (C) quit        (D) eliminate

_____ 11. The library is very quiet with only an _____ cough from the students or the movement of a chair.

    (A) urgent        (B) agreeable        (C) occasional        (D) essential

_____ 12. Most of the soldiers carried _____ bags.

    (A) canyon        (B) canoe        (C) cape        (D) canvas

_____ 13. I need a pair of _____. I want to cut the string.

    (A) stockings        (B) scissors        (C) socks        (D) pants

_____ 14. He worked _____ to achieve his goal of being a great scientist.

    (A) feverishly        (B) tiredly        (C) fruitlessly        (D) reluctantly

_____ 15. I cannot help myself _____ at the letter to see what the teacher has told my parents about me.

    (A) gazing         (B) peeping         (C) staring         (D) glancing

_____ 16. I'm burning with _____ —you must tell me who has won the game at last.

    (A) fire         (B) curiosity         (C) stove         (D) electricity

_____ 17. Our restaurant has just managed to survive; we don't know when it will become _____.

    (A) beneficial         (B) profitable         (C) advantageous         (D) financial

_____ 18. She is pursuing her life goal with _____. Thus, I believe she will succeed someday.

    (A) flattery         (B) integration         (C) determination         (D) structure

_____ 19. The _____ caused by the recent typhoon has killed dozens of people and left many more homeless.

    (A) landlord         (B) landscape         (C) landslide         (D) landmine

_____ 20. Mother Teresa _____ all her life to the care of the poor and homeless people.

    (A) donated         (B) selected         (C) devoted         (D) departed

## II. Idioms & Phrases

_____ 1. I _____ my math lessons in the hope of getting good grades.

    (A) got tired of                 (B) had great trouble in

    (C) took great pains with         (D) gave rise to

_____ 2. Before going to Germany, I suggest you _____ your German.

    (A) brush up         (B) hang up         (C) put up         (D) show up

_____ 3. With proper first aid and medical care, the wounded soldier _____.

    (A) came to life         (B) brought to life         (C) took his life         (D) risked his life

_____ 4. By hard working, his financial status seemed to be improving _____.

    (A) by far         (B) by degrees         (C) by the dozen         (D) by the way

_____ 5. It _____ that you will be thrown out if you don't pay the rent.

    (A) makes believe              (B) makes no difference

    (C) stands at attention         (D) stands to reason

_____ 6. The bookshelf was _____ the wall.

    (A) set up         (B) built into         (C) put off         (D) piled up

_____ 7. He is wearing a jacket which _____ bullets so he won't get hurt by gun shots.

    (A) is decorated with             (B) is resistant to

    (C) is made of                (D) is provided with

8. I am too busy to cook, so I have to _____.

(A) carry out      (B) keep alive      (C) dine out      (D) get through

9. The hunters _____ in a cave when they were caught in a storm.

(A) took refuge      (B) took steps      (C) played fair      (D) lighted up

10. After walking for an hour, I'm _____ a cup of iced tea now.

(A) dying away      (B) dying for      (C) dying out      (D) dying from

## III. Cloze Test

### Part A

A pleasant smile is a strong indication of a friendly and open attitude and a(n) ___1___ to communicate. It is a positive, nonverbal signal sent with the hope that the other person will smile, and you ___2___ that you have noticed the person in a positive manner. The other person considers it a ___3___ and will usually feel good. The result is the other person will usually smile back.

Smiling does not mean that you have to put on a phony face or ___4___ that you are happy all of the time. But when you see someone you know, or would like to ___5___ him/her, do smile.

1. (A) willingness      (B) objection      (C) refusal      (D) hatred

2. (A) discover      (B) demonstrate      (C) pretend      (D) defend

3. (A) complaint      (B) compliment      (C) composition      (D) comparison

4. (A) predict      (B) pretend      (C) prefer      (D) prevent

5. (A) make fun of      (B) lose touch with

     (C) look down upon      (D) make contact with

### Part B

You might not realize that closed posture is the cause of many conversational problems. ___1___ closed posture is sitting with your arms and legs crossed and your hand ___2___ your mouth or chin. This is often called "thinking pose," but just ask yourself this question: Are you going to interrupt someone who ___3___ to be deep in thought? Not only does this posture ___4___ "stay away" signal to others, but it also prevents your main "signal sender" (your mouth) from being seen by others looking for receptive conversational signals. ___5___ these receptive signals, another person will most likely avoid you and look for someone who appears to be more available for contact.

1. (A) Typical      (B) Peculiar      (C) Unknown      (D) Exceptional

2. (A) scratching      (B) revealing      (C) directing      (D) covering

3. (A) applies      (B) appears      (C) approves      (D) appeals

_____ 4. (A) give off      (B) wear away      (C) count on      (D) head for

_____ 5. (A) In case of      (B) In spite of      (C) Without      (D) As a result of

## Part C

Most mothers have a good piece of advice: Never go into a supermarket _____1____! If you go shopping for food before lunchtime, you'll probably buy more than you plan to. ____2____, however, just this simple advice isn't enough for consumers these days. Modern ____3____ need an education in how—and ____4____—to buy things at the grocery store. First, you should check out the weekly newspaper ____5____. Find out the items that are on sale and decide if you really need those things. ____6____, don't buy anything just because it's cheaper than usual. ____7____, in the market, carefully read the information on the ____8____, and don't let words like "New and Improved" or "All Natural" on the front of a package ____9____ you. Instead, read the list of ingredients on the back. ____10____, compare prices; that is, you should examine the prices both of different brands and different sizes of the same brand.

_____ 1. (A) hungry      (B) hot      (C) humiliated      (D) hurried

_____ 2. (A) Fortunately      (B) Fortune      (C) Unfortunately      (D) Misfortune

_____ 3. (A) grocers      (B) pupils      (C) shoppers      (D) secretaries

_____ 4. (A) how to      (B) how long      (C) how many      (D) how not

_____ 5. (A) ads      (B) AIDS      (C) headlines      (D) comics

_____ 6. (A) In other words                 (B) As a result

        (C) In case                      (D) On the other hand

_____ 7. (A) Last      (B) Most importantly      (C) To start with      (D) Next

_____ 8. (A) surface      (B) skin      (C) front page      (D) package

_____ 9. (A) invade      (B) invest      (C) influence      (D) investigate

_____ 10. (A) By contrast      (B) Third      (C) To conclude      (D) For example

完成日期：_____

實戰語錄

*A good tale is none the worse for being told twice.*

舊書不厭百回讀。

## Round 1

I. 1. A  2. A  3. D  4. B  5. D  6. C  7. B  8. A  9. D  10. C
   11. D  12. B  13. D  14. B  15. D  16. A  17. B  18. C  19. C  20. B
II. 1. B  2. A  3. A  4. A  5. C  6. B  7. A  8. C  9. D  10. D
III. (A) 1. D  2. C  3. A  4. A  5. D  6. C  7. D  8. A  9. D  10. A
    (B) 1. D  2. B  3. A  4. C  5. A  6. C  7. D  8. D  9. B  10. A

## Round 2

I. 1. D  2. C  3. A  4. C  5. B  6. B  7. B  8. A  9. A  10. A
   11. D  12. C  13. A  14. C  15. C  16. B  17. C  18. A  19. C  20. C
II. 1. C  2. B  3. B  4. D  5. B  6. A  7. C  8. B  9. B  10. D
III. (A) 1. A  2. B  3. C  4. D  5. C  6. C  7. A  8. A  9. D  10. D
    (B) 1. B  2. A  3. C  4. A  5. D  6. B  7. A  8. D  9. B  10. C

## Round 3

I. 1. B  2. B  3. C  4. A  5. D  6. D  7. C  8. D  9. B  10. C
   11. D  12. C  13. C  14. B  15. C  16. A  17. B  18. C  19. C  20. C
II. 1. D  2. C  3. B  4. B  5. A  6. A  7. B  8. A  9. A  10. B
III. (A) 1. B  2. C  3. A  4. A  5. C  6. D  7. D  8. B  9. A  10. C
    (B) 1. B  2. A  3. A  4. D  5. C
    (C) 1. B  2. D  3. A  4. C  5. A

## Round 4

I. 1. C  2. B  3. B  4. A  5. B  6. C  7. C  8. B  9. B  10. D
   11. D  12. D  13. A  14. B  15. B  16. B  17. B  18. A  19. C  20. A
II. 1. C  2. C  3. D  4. C  5. C  6. D  7. B  8. A  9. B  10. B
III. 1. C  2. D  3. A  4. A  5. B  6. C  7. A  8. D  9. B  10. B
    11. A  12. C  13. D  14. A  15. B  16. C  17. C  18. B  19. A  20. D

## Round 5

I. 1. A  2. A  3. B  4. D  5. C  6. C  7. D  8. A  9. C  10. C
   11. B  12. A  13. C  14. B  15. A  16. A  17. C  18. B  19. A  20. C

II. 1. C　2. D　3. B　4. B　5. D　6. C　7. B　8. A　9. A　10. C
III. (A) 1. A　2. B　3. D　4. C　5. C　6. D　7. A　8. B　9. C　10. A
　　(B) 1. C　2. D　3. A　4. D　5. B　6. A　7. C　8. B　9. D　10. B

## Round 6

I. 1. D　2. D　3. B　4. A　5. A　6. A　7. C　8. C　9. A　10. A
　11. A　12. B　13. C　14. B　15. D　16. B　17. C　18. B　19. B　20. D
II. 1. B　2. B　3. B　4. D　5. C　6. B　7. A　8. B　9. C　10. B
III. (A) 1. B　2. A　3. D　4. D　5. A　6. C　7. C　8. A　9. D　10. B
　　(B) 1. C　2. D　3. D　4. C　5. B　6. A　7. C　8. C　9. D　10. A

## Round 7

I. 1. C　2. A　3. C　4. C　5. B　6. C　7. A　8. A　9. A　10. D
　11. C　12. B　13. D　14. B　15. A　16. D　17. C　18. A　19. A　20. B
II. 1. D　2. A　3. D　4. A　5. B　6. A　7. C　8. B　9. D　10. B
III. (A) 1. D　2. A　3. C　4. D　5. D　6. C　7. A　8. D　9. B　10. D
　　(B) 1. D　2. C　3. A　4. A　5. B　6. D　7. C　8. C　9. A　10. B

## Round 8

I. 1. B　2. D　3. D　4. C　5. C　6. B　7. D　8. D　9. D　10. A
　11. C　12. C　13. D　14. C　15. B　16. C　17. A　18. C　19. C　20. B
II. 1. A　2. D　3. C　4. D　5. D　6. A　7. A　8. B　9. B　10. A
III. (A) 1. C　2. D　3. B　4. B　5. A　6. D　7. D　8. A　9. B　10. D
　　(B) 1. B　2. D　3. A　4. C　5. C　6. D　7. A　8. A　9. B　10. C

## Round 9

I. 1. A　2. D　3. D　4. B　5. B　6. B　7. C　8. D　9. D　10. D
　11. C　12. A　13. D　14. D　15. A　16. A　17. C　18. A　19. D　20. D
II. 1. B　2. C　3. B　4. C　5. A　6. D　7. A　8. B　9. C　10. B
III. (A) 1. A　2. C　3. B　4. C　5. D　6. A　7. A　8. B　9. D　10. B
　　(B) 1. A　2. C　3. B　4. D　5. A　6. A　7. A　8. B　9. D　10. D

## Round 10

I. 1. A　2. C　3. B　4. D　5. C　6. B　7. B　8. D　9. A　10. C
　11. D　12. B　13. A　14. A　15. A　16. C　17. B　18. D　19. C　20. B

II. 1. A   2. C   3. D   4. C   5. B   6. A   7. C   8. A   9. B   10. A
III. (A) 1. C   2. D   3. B   4. D   5. A   6. C   7. B   8. B   9. D   10. A
    (B) 1. B   2. B   3. D   4. A   5. B   6. A   7. C   8. D   9. C   10. B

## Round 11

I. 1. D   2. C   3. C   4. B   5. D   6. C   7. A   8. C   9. C   10. B
   11. A   12. A   13. C   14. C   15. D   16. B   17. A   18. C   19. A   20. A
II. 1. D   2. A   3. B   4. C   5. B   6. C   7. C   8. C   9. C   10. B
III. (A) 1. D   2. D   3. A   4. D   5. B   6. B   7. A   8. A   9. C   10. C
    (B) 1. B   2. A   3. C   4. D   5. D   6. B   7. B   8. A   9. B   10. C

## Round 12

I. 1. A   2. B   3. B   4. A   5. D   6. C   7. D   8. A   9. B   10. A
   11. A   12. B   13. C   14. B   15. D   16. D   17. A   18. B   19. C   20. D
II. 1. D   2. B   3. B   4. D   5. D   6. A   7. A   8. B   9. C   10. A
III. (A) 1. D   2. C   3. B   4. B   5. A   6. C   7. A   8. D   9. D   10. A
    (B) 1. B   2. B   3. D   4. A   5. C   6. B   7. A   8. D   9. D   10. B

## Round 13

I. 1. C   2. A   3. D   4. C   5. C   6. B   7. B   8. C   9. A   10. D
   11. A   12. D   13. D   14. B   15. D   16. C   17. D   18. B   19. B   20. B
II. 1. B   2. A   3. C   4. C   5. D   6. C   7. B   8. C   9. D   10. C
III. (A) 1. A   2. B   3. D   4. A   5. B   6. C   7. D   8. C   9. A   10. D
    (B) 1. D   2. A   3. B   4. C   5. D   6. A   7. A   8. D   9. D   10. C

## Round 14

I. 1. B   2. C   3. A   4. D   5. A   6. D   7. B   8. D   9. A   10. D
   11. D   12. D   13. B   14. C   15. D   16. B   17. A   18. B   19. C   20. C
II. 1. B   2. C   3. D   4. B   5. A   6. A   7. C   8. B   9. B   10. A
III. (A) 1. A   2. A   3. D   4. B   5. B   6. D   7. A   8. D   9. C   10. A
    (B) 1. C   2. A   3. B   4. A   5. C   6. D   7. A   8. D   9. C   10. D

## Round 15

I. 1. A   2. B   3. A   4. B   5. C   6. C   7. A   8. B   9. C   10. B
   11. D   12. A   13. C   14. A   15. D   16. B   17. C   18. A   19. A   20. C

II. 1. B   2. B   3. A   4. C   5. D   6. A   7. B   8. D   9. C   10. A
III. (A) 1. D   2. A   3. B   4. C   5. D   6. A   7. A   8. B   9. C   10. D
   (B) 1. D   2. C   3. B   4. A   5. A   6. D   7. A   8. C   9. B   10. D

## Round 16

I. 1. D   2. C   3. B   4. A   5. C   6. B   7. B   8. A   9. D   10. D
   11. D   12. C   13. D   14. D   15. B   16. D   17. C   18. C   19. A   20. A
II. 1. C   2. D   3. B   4. C   5. A   6. A   7. D   8. D   9. C   10. D
III. (A) 1. B   2. A   3. D   4. D   5. C   6. B   7. B   8. D   9. A   10. B
   (B) 1. A   2. D   3. D   4. B   5. B   6. A   7. C   8. D   9. B   10. C

## Round 17

I. 1. A   2. D   3. C   4. C   5. A   6. A   7. B   8. D   9. D   10. B
   11. D   12. C   13. A   14. D   15. C   16. A   17. D   18. C   19. B   20. D
II. 1. A   2. D   3. B   4. B   5. A   6. D   7. B   8. B   9. C   10. A
III. (A) 1. C   2. D   3. A   4. A   5. C   6. B   7. B   8. B   9. B   10. D
   (B) 1. C   2. B   3. A   4. D   5. D   6. D   7. C   8. C   9. B   10. A

## Round 18

I. 1. D   2. A   3. D   4. B   5. D   6. D   7. C   8. A   9. D   10. D
   11. A   12. B   13. D   14. C   15. C   16. A   17. C   18. B   19. C   20. D
II. 1. A   2. D   3. D   4. C   5. A   6. B   7. C   8. C   9. B   10. C
III. (A) 1. A   2. D   3. B   4. C   5. D   6. A   7. B   8. B   9. A   10. C
   (B) 1. A   2. C   3. B   4. A   5. A   6. D   7. A   8. A   9. C   10. D

## Round 19

I. 1. B   2. B   3. A   4. D   5. C   6. C   7. C   8. D   9. A   10. A
   11. D   12. A   13. C   14. A   15. C   16. C   17. D   18. B   19. C   20. C
II. 1. C   2. B   3. B   4. B   5. D   6. A   7. D   8. B   9. B   10. D
III. (A) 1. D   2. A   3. B   4. C   5. C   6. D   7. A   8. D   9. B   10. C
   (B) 1. A   2. B   3. A   4. D   5. B   6. B   7. B   8. A   9. C   10. C

## Round 20

I. 1. A   2. C   3. D   4. A   5. B   6. B   7. A   8. A   9. D   10. C
   11. C   12. B   13. B   14. C   15. D   16. D   17. A   18. D   19. C   20. B

II. 1. B  2. B  3. A  4. D  5. B  6. A  7. A  8. A  9. C  10. A
III. (A) 1. A  2. B  3. C  4. C  5. B  6. C  7. A  8. A  9. D  10. B
   (B) 1. A  2. C  3. C  4. B  5. A  6. A  7. D  8. D  9. B  10. C

## Round 21

I. 1. D  2. A  3. B  4. C  5. D  6. C  7. A  8. C  9. C  10. B
   11. C  12. D  13. B  14. B  15. B  16. B  17. C  18. A  19. B  20. A
II. 1. A  2. A  3. C  4. D  5. B  6. D  7. A  8. A  9. C  10. B
III. (A) 1. C  2. D  3. A  4. B  5. D
   (B) 1. B  2. C  3. C  4. D  5. D
   (C) 1. B  2. A  3. C  4. D  5. C  6. C  7. C  8. A  9. D  10. A

## Round 22

I. 1. C  2. A  3. B  4. A  5. C  6. B  7. A  8. D  9. D  10. A
   11. C  12. C  13. D  14. D  15. B  16. C  17. C  18. C  19. A  20. A
II. 1. D  2. A  3. B  4. C  5. B  6. A  7. C  8. D  9. B  10. C
III. (A) 1. B  2. A  3. B  4. B  5. B  6. A  7. D  8. A  9. C  10. D
   (B) 1. B  2. A  3. C  4. A  5. D  6. C  7. B  8. C  9. C  10. B

## Round 23

I. 1. D  2. A  3. D  4. B  5. D  6. D  7. B  8. C  9. D  10. A
   11. C  12. A  13. B  14. B  15. A  16. D  17. B  18. D  19. D  20. D
II. 1. D  2. B  3. A  4. A  5. A  6. A  7. C  8. A  9. C  10. B
III. (A) 1. B  2. D  3. B  4. A  5. D
   (B) 1. D  2. B  3. D  4. D  5. A
   (C) 1. B  2. B  3. D  4. C  5. A  6. A  7. B  8. A  9. C  10. B

## Round 24

I. 1. A  2. C  3. C  4. D  5. A  6. C  7. B  8. B  9. D  10. D
   11. C  12. D  13. D  14. C  15. B  16. B  17. B  18. D  19. A  20. D
II. 1. A  2. C  3. B  4. C  5. A  6. B  7. D  8. D  9. B  10. C
III. (A) 1. B  2. C  3. B  4. D  5. D  6. D  7. D  8. B  9. A  10. A
   (B) 1. A  2. B  3. D  4. B  5. C  6. A  7. D  8. A  9. B  10. C

## Round 25

I. 1. A   2. C   3. A   4. B   5. A   6. D   7. B   8. A   9. D   10. B
  11. B   12. B   13. D   14. A   15. D   16. B   17. C   18. A   19. A   20. C
II. 1. B   2. C   3. C   4. B   5. A   6. A   7. C   8. A   9. D   10. B
III. (A) 1. A   2. C   3. D   4. A   5. A   6. D   7. C   8. B   9. A   10. D
  (B) 1. A   2. A   3. C   4. C   5. A   6. B   7. A   8. C   9. C   10. B

## Round 26

I. 1. B   2. C   3. C   4. A   5. C   6. A   7. A   8. B   9. C   10. C
  11. B   12. B   13. A   14. D   15. C   16. A   17. C   18. D   19. C   20. B
II. 1. A   2. D   3. B   4. C   5. A   6. C   7. C   8. D   9. D   10. B
III. (A) 1. A   2. D   3. B   4. D   5. A   6. C   7. C   8. B   9. C   10. A
  (B) 1. B   2. A   3. C   4. A   5. D   6. B   7. D   8. A   9. C   10. A

## Round 27

I. 1. C   2. C   3. B   4. D   5. A   6. B   7. D   8. C   9. C   10. D
  11. B   12. B   13. D   14. A   15. B   16. B   17. A   18. C   19. C   20. D
II. 1. B   2. D   3. D   4. A   5. B   6. A   7. A   8. A   9. C   10. A
III. (A) 1. A   2. B   3. D   4. B   5. C   6. C   7. D   8. C   9. A   10. B
  (B) 1. B   2. B   3. C   4. B   5. A   6. C   7. A   8. D   9. D   10. C

## Round 28

I. 1. D   2. B   3. A   4. B   5. D   6. D   7. D   8. D   9. B   10. A
  11. B   12. A   13. B   14. A   15. D   16. C   17. D   18. B   19. C   20. A
II. 1. B   2. D   3. B   4. A   5. B   6. C   7. A   8. C   9. D   10. A
III. (A) 1. B   2. B   3. C   4. A   5. D   6. A   7. C   8. D   9. D   10. A
  (B) 1. A   2. A   3. D   4. B   5. C   6. B   7. D   8. D   9. B   10. B

## Round 29

I. 1. A   2. C   3. C   4. C   5. D   6. D   7. B   8. B   9. D   10. D
  11. D   12. A   13. C   14. B   15. C   16. A   17. A   18. B   19. A   20. A
II. 1. C   2. C   3. D   4. D   5. B   6. B   7. A   8. D   9. B   10. D
III. (A) 1. A   2. D   3. B   4. C   5. B   6. B   7. A   8. D   9. D   10. A
  (B) 1. C   2. B   3. D   4. D   5. B   6. B   7. C   8. B   9. D   10. D

## Round 30

I. 1. D  2. D  3. D  4. C  5. B  6. B  7. A  8. A  9. A  10. D
  11. C  12. D  13. B  14. A  15. B  16. B  17. B  18. C  19. C  20. C
II. 1. C  2. A  3. A  4. B  5. D  6. B  7. B  8. C  9. A  10. B
III. (A) 1. A  2. B  3. B  4. B  5. D
  (B) 1. A  2. D  3. B  4. A  5. C
  (C) 1. A  2. C  3. C  4. D  5. A  6. A  7. D  8. D  9. C  10. B

# 學測英文混合題實戰演練

溫宥基　編著

## 新型學測 混合題 完全攻略
## 打造 最強解題 技巧

◆ **混合題閱讀策略大公開**

全書共 14 單元，第 1 至 2 單元為「策略篇」，

介紹閱讀技巧及命題核心，

同步搭配應用練習，有效掌握閱讀策略與答題技巧。

◆ **訓練混合題型實戰能力**

第 3 至 14 單元為「實戰篇」，

每單元一篇混合題題組，

題型含多選、填表、簡答、單詞填空、圖片配合題等，

精熟學測出題模式。

◆ **附文章中譯和詳盡解析**

解析結合策略篇應試邏輯，進一步強化解題思維、

內化作答要點。

# 20分鐘稱霸 大考英文作文

王靖賢 編著

- 共16回作文練習，涵蓋大考作文3大題型：看圖寫作、主題寫作、信函寫作。根據近年大考趨勢精心出題，題型多元且擬真度高。

- 每回作文練習皆有為考生精選的英文名言佳句，增強考生備考戰力。

- 附方便攜帶的解析本，針對每回作文題目提供寫作架構圖，讓寫作脈絡一目了然，並提供範文、寫作要點、寫作撇步及好用詞彙，一本在手即可增強英文作文能力。

# 學測英文字彙力 6000 PLUS⁺ 隨身讀

三民英語編輯小組　彙整

## 第一本 完整收錄最新字表的隨身讀！
## 獨家贈送「拼讀」音檔，用聽的也能背單字！

### 本書特色

◆ **符合學測範圍！**

依據「高中英文參考詞彙表（111 學年度起適用）」編寫，收錄 Level 1–6 字彙及 PLUS 實力延伸字彙，共 250 回，掌握學測字彙，應戰各類考試。

◆ **拼讀音檔！**

專業外籍錄音員錄製，音檔採「拼讀」模式（success，s-u-c-c-e-s-s，success，成功），用聽覺輔助記憶。

◆ **補充詳盡！**

補充常用搭配詞、同反義字及片語，有利舉一反三、輕鬆延伸學習範圍。

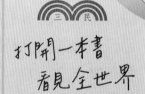